Suddenly Theresa's world was a terrifying place. Shy, uncertain, and sure that her dark skin made her dumb, she was not at all prepared to cope with her mother's death and her placement in a foster home.

The Chintons were kind people but, unlike her precious ivy plant, Theresa seemed unable to adjust to her new surroundings. Then slowly, without knowing exactly what was happening and without meaning to, Theresa began to get involved with new friends and new situations. And all at once she found herself, not running away, but fighting in the way she thought best for her new friends and for something that was very important.

A NEW HOME FOR THERESA deals with integration, but more than that it warmly and sympathetically deals with a girl's difficult adjustment to inevitable changes in her life and her growth as a person. James Barkley's sensitive illustrations catch Theresa's moods and feelings and evoke a very real picture of sadness, warmth, and transition.

A New Home For Theresa

Illustrated by James Barkley

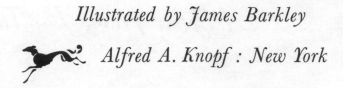 *Alfred A. Knopf : New York*

A New Home For Theresa / Betty Baum

To my grandchildren:

Julie,

Dena,

Laura,

Jonathan,

Sharon,

Theodore

A New Home For Theresa

One

Theresa's mother was sick. On the bed they shared, Theresa had piled everything in the apartment that might keep her mother warm. A pillow toppled off her mother's trembling feet.

"May I go down to Mrs. Gardiner and borrow a blanket?" Theresa begged timidly. "You haven't stopped shaking and coughing all night long."

Mrs. Ellmsby shut her eyes. "Don't bother anybody. I'm all right."

Theresa picked up the pillow and laid it across her mother's feet. When she stopped coughing, Theresa's mother pointed to the clock. "School!" she said.

"Mama, not today," Theresa pleaded. "It won't matter. I don't learn much anyway."

Her mother pulled herself partway into a sitting position. "See, I'm fine. Nothing the matter with me. Just a bad cold. I always have a cold, first thing in the fall. Sixth grade is important . . ." Another fit of coughing shook her body.

"I'll get the cough medicine," Theresa whispered. Never had her mother been this tired from a cold . . .

The cough syrup had been used up. Theresa caught her breath. Would her mother let her ask for credit? Or borrow money from Mrs. Gardiner?

"First, I'll give Mama her coffee, then I'll ask if I can borrow some money, or ask the druggist for credit," she said to herself. It was not easy talking about money to her mother. Even when her mother was well, such talk gave her a sick headache. Theresa thought about the words she might use to make the subject less painful for them both.

Theresa put a pot of water on to boil. She measured out the instant coffee, enough for breakfast and an extra cup for her mother to drink midmorning.

She did not look in the refrigerator. She knew there was no milk, and she decided they would have coffee without it. They still had a few slices of bread, a quarter of a jar of coffee, and some sugar. Somehow she would have to get money. Would her mother be able to go to work tomorrow?

Theresa listened to the sound of her mother's irregular breathing. With her mother as sick as this, how could she be thinking of money?

Nervously, Theresa wandered over to the window sill. The Gardiners lived directly below them. Maybe Mrs. Gardiner would come upstairs. She must have heard Theresa walking around all night, and her mother's coughing.

Idly she fingered the ivy plant on the sill. The long, almost leafless vine was a disordered tangle. She lifted it to the light.

"You need help, too," she murmured. "I'm getting real scared . . . "

Her mother began to cough again. Theresa dropped the vine on the sill and ran into the bedroom. "Mama," she cried. "Mama, please let me get Mrs. Gardiner."

Theresa wiped her mother's face. The brown skin seemed transparent. "Please, Mama," Theresa said. "Or let me go down to the drugstore. The druggist'll trust me. He always trusts the Gardiners. I'll get aspirins and cough medicine."

Tears rolled down her mother's cheeks. Theresa brushed them away. Softly, soothingly, she whispered, "Don't cry, Mama. I won't talk about taking credit. I'm not scared any more." She wrapped her arms around her mother and held on to her tightly.

Theresa's mother kissed her. "Go to the shop after school. Ask the boss to give you some work. I can sew in bed."

"Mama, I went yesterday. He isn't allowed to give out work to minors. You must come for the work yourself. Or maybe Mrs. Gardiner could come with me." Theresa spoke gently as she adjusted the pillow under her mother's head. "I'll get the coffee now. We'll both feel better after some coffee."

Her mother drank slowly from the cup Theresa held for her. Color returned to her face. "Now drink your coffee and go to school," Mrs. Ellmsby said softly. "See, I'm much better. All I needed was a hot cup of coffee."

Theresa drank her coffee. Her mother did seem better, and when she pointed to the clock, Theresa went for her school books.

"Take your sweater," Mrs. Ellmsby said. She tried to find it among the bedclothes.

Theresa found her thin, faded sweater and slipped it around her mother's shoulders.

"I won't need the sweater. It's the middle of September. Still summer."

"I heard the wind yesterday and I can feel from the draft coming through the window that it's cold . . . We'll have to get more cardboard to cover the window until we can get it fixed so it will close." Mrs. Ellmsby began to shake again.

Theresa ran to her mother's side. "Please let me stay home today."

Mrs. Ellmsby's eyes were steady. "I can manage," she said firmly.

When her mother looked at her this way, it was best to obey without questioning. She wished there were a relative she might call, but there was no one. Her father had died of a heart attack before she was born. Mrs. Ellmsby had taken up millinery because she could bring work home. She had never left Theresa with anyone. Only when Theresa had begun to go to school full time had her mother gone to work in a factory. "My great big girl," her mother had called her when she had hung the key to the apartment around Theresa's neck.

If I'm a great big girl, I better think of some way to get money, Theresa thought as she brushed her hair without looking in the mirror.

Her friend Laura Gardiner had suggested she go to the city Welfare office. Laura was sure that the Ellmsbys could get a monthly check for food and rent. When someone in the Gardiner family was sick, Welfare provided extra money for doctor bills and medicine.

Theresa bent over her mother. She formed what she would say in her mind. But when her mother's eyes met hers, not a word about going to Welfare would come out.

Mrs. Ellmsby said hoarsely, "Eight-thirty, darling."

Theresa kissed her mother. Mrs. Ellmsby tugged loose the sweater. "Take it. I'm not cold," she said.

"Neither am I," Theresa replied, and she put her mother's hands back under the covers. Her face brightened. "Mama," she added as she turned to go for her books, "I think the draft from the window is hurting the ivy. Remember how pretty it was when I gave it to you on Mother's Day? Well, I think I'm going to ask Mrs. Gardiner to come up sometime this morning to look at the poor plant. I'm going to leave her my key, so don't get scared if you hear someone coming into the apartment."

She scooped up her books from the table and ran out of the apartment. Her mother could not be angry if Mrs. Gardiner came up to look at the plant. She had not really told a lie, she told herself. The plant really did

look more than half dead.

On the fourth-floor landing, three of the Gardiners were waiting. Mrs. Gardiner stopped buttoning the youngest Gardiner's coat.

"Tweedy, I heard your mother coughing all night long. When are you going to call a doctor?" Mrs. Gardiner asked.

Theresa began to fumble with her books. "We have no money. You know how my mother is about taking credit."

Mrs. Gardiner clicked her tongue disapprovingly. She finished buttoning Cookie's coat before she said, "Too much pride is sometimes foolish. Your mother sounds very sick."

Theresa's eyes met the older woman's gaze. "Please," she said falteringly. "You know how my mother likes to keep to herself . . . but, would you . . . could you . . . if you have time this morning . . . could you go upstairs and . . . and look at my ivy plant. I'm afraid something is going to happen to it."

Mrs. Gardiner took the key from Theresa's outstretched hand. "I'll go upstairs, child. More than once. Don't worry. If I can talk some sense into her, I will."

She held on to Theresa's hand for a moment. "Let me find a coat or a sweater for you. It's colder today than it was yesterday," she said.

Theresa smiled as she had been taught to do. "No, thank you," she sang out as she ran down the stairs with Cookie and Laura behind her. "I'm never cold."

The three girls walked quickly and close together. A strong wind whipped around the corners, sending shivers through Theresa. It raced over the open garbage cans.

"Look at the garbage flying around," Theresa said, to keep her goose-pimpled arms from being the topic of conversation. She faked a laugh and added, "Instead of carrying that garbage, the wind ought to try carrying us. It could sweep us all the way to school."

Cookie clung to Theresa's skirt. "The wind is blowing me too much already. I want the wind to stop."

Theresa ran the last block. School had never looked more inviting! She hurried into the line-up yard and willingly got in line.

Her teacher, Mrs. Burns, was on duty. She came over to Theresa, a worried frown creasing her forehead.

"Haven't you a coat, or a warm sweater?" Mrs. Burns asked Theresa softly.

Theresa lowered her head. Mrs. Burns lifted Theresa's chin gently. "There's nothing shameful about being poor, Tessie. Please come with me to the PTA storage closet after lunch. I'm sure we can find something warm to fit you."

Theresa pulled away. Theresa knew that Mrs. Burns meant to be kind and Theresa did not mean to be rude, but she did not know how to explain to the teacher that she did not want a handout. Her mother would never let her wear anyone else's old clothing.

Mrs. Burns said, "No child can be expected to learn if she's cold or hungry."

Theresa found her voice. "I'm not hungry," she mumbled. She glanced around to see whether Laura or anyone else had heard Mrs. Burns.

Laura had walked Cookie to the first-grade line. She now pushed her way into the space directly behind Theresa. Okay? Laura asked with her eyes.

Theresa nodded and looked away from her teacher. Mrs. Burns asked Theresa to step over to the side. Theresa said softly, "I don't need anything."

Mrs. Burns' face reddened and she turned and walked toward one of the other class lines. Her feelings were obviously hurt. Theresa was sorry about this and hoped Mrs. Burns would not act snippy to get even.

In the classroom Theresa sat low in her seat. She expected Mrs. Burns to snap at her the first chance she got. Theresa had had snippy teachers before and expected to have them again. She had learned how to keep smiling until the teacher got over her anger.

But Mrs. Burns said nothing to her. Theresa kept the smile on her face and avoided everyone's eyes. The room was quiet and warm. She did not know when her head drooped down to the desk and her eyes closed. It was not until ten to twelve when the lunch bell rang that she knew she had fallen asleep in class.

Mrs. Burns was standing beside her desk. "Theresa, Laura told me all about your mother. If your mother isn't better when you get home, perhaps you could get her to go to the clinic. I wrote down the name of the one nearest your house."

Mrs. Burns handed Theresa a slip of paper and then reached for her purse. "Will you need money for carfare?"

Theresa did not wait to hear another word. The force of her anger carried her straight out of the classroom, down the stairs, and all the way home.

What had made her teacher think her a beggar? She ran home without waiting for Cookie and Laura. Up the stairs she ran, and she stopped only when she saw that the door to her apartment was wide open.

"Ma," Theresa called silently. She took a deep breath and waited until her lips stopped trembling. She had been taught not to talk about her troubles in front of strangers. She was not even allowed to complain when she and her mother were alone together. Complaints about teachers, other children, or hunger could not be fixed, so why talk about them!

She summoned up a smile and stepped into the kitchen. "Mrs. Gardiner? Did you come to see about my plant?"

Mrs. Gardiner came out of the bedroom. "Tweedy, child, I hate to tell you this, but I think your mother is worse. Don't cry, honey. I think she has a fever. I'll stay with her while you go down to the druggist and ask him to call an ambulance."

Theresa crossed her fingers and went into the bedroom. Her mother was lying as if asleep. Her breathing had become noisier and faster than it had been that morning.

"I can't call an ambulance. My mother will be angry. I have to listen to my mother," Theresa mumbled. "She didn't want me to call you, so how can I call an ambulance?"

Mrs. Gardiner's face made Theresa's heart beat faster and faster. She had never disobeyed her mother. Her mother wanted her to "take what comes without crying." Was going for an ambulance taking what comes?

A pain shot through Theresa; way up into her head it reached. The longer she looked at Mrs. Gardiner's worried face, the more frightened she became.

The door of the apartment was still open. That seemed the only way out of her problem. Without a word, she rushed out of the kitchen, down the stairs, and past the children coming home from school.

She looked for a place to hide. She found it. Her old hiding place under the steps. She crept into the darkness and sat there, too frightened even to cry.

Two

A few minutes later, Laura found her. "Tweedy, my mother sent me to call the ambulance. I just did."

Theresa came out into the light. "I wish I could stop myself from running away when I'm scared."

Laura took her hand. "Lucky I remembered where you used to hide when we played hide-and-seek. How long would you have stayed here?"

"I don't know," Theresa said miserably. "I guess I'm a coward. My mother says people never change . . ." She looked at Laura. "Did you see her? I'm so scared . . ."

"The ambulance will be here soon. Let's go up and

wait," Laura said in her ordinary voice.

Theresa walked slowly up the stairs. She felt torn between wishing that her mother would be sitting up and ready to scold her for letting Mrs. Gardiner have the key to their apartment and wishing that her mother would still be too sleepy to care about Mrs. Gardiner or the ambulance. By the time she decided that she would prefer the scolding, the ambulance doctor was in the house.

"Pneumonia," the doctor told Mrs. Gardiner and Theresa.

Mrs. Ellmsby did not wake up when she was put on the stretcher. Mrs. Gardiner asked if Val, her oldest daughter, who had just come home from school, could go with Theresa in the ambulance.

The doctor said, after some thought, "Yes, Theresa *is* far too young to travel to and from the hospital alone. She should have someone with her."

Two hours later, Theresa and Val came back to the Gardiner apartment. Val had done all the talking at the hospital.

"Lucky for me you had only a half day of school today," Theresa said to Val as she walked toward the door to leave.

Mrs. Gardiner stopped her. "Better for you to sleep down here, Tweedy. You can't stay alone upstairs. Get your pajamas; you can share the bed with Cookie and Laura. Won't hurt for a few days."

Val, with the practicality of an eighteen-year-old, suggested that *she* sleep in the bed upstairs, but Mrs. Gardiner said it was impossible. The bed could not be used until the sheets had been washed and the room aired.

"Can I go upstairs and do my homework? It's a shame to let such a big, quiet kitchen go to waste," Val said to Theresa later that afternoon.

Theresa was glad to do something for Val. She gave up her key willingly.

In the Gardiner apartment all six children put themselves out to make Theresa feel at home. Benjy and Bethina, the twins, entertained her with stories about their junior high school. Not one of the stories was complimentary.

Mrs. Gardiner looked sharply at Benjy. "Bad as the schools are, I'd have been glad to go to a school half that good. In my day we didn't get a chance to go to school. When I was ten I went to work."

Tony Gardiner stretched to his full sixteen-year-old length. "I wish I had lived in those days. I'd rather go to work than go to any rotten old school."

Mrs. Gardiner wrapped the towel she was holding around Tony's head. Theresa had to laugh at the make-believe fight Tony was having with his mother and the towel. The four younger Gardiners joined in the play.

I wish I had a big family, Theresa thought as she sat and watched.

Val came down from Theresa's apartment after she finished her homework. As soon as she walked into the room, she asked what the noise was all about.

"Tony," Val said as she helped unscramble him from the kids on top of him, "you'd like school as much as I do if you applied yourself and got good marks."

Tony made a face. "Look who's talking! You've always been good in school. No wonder you're going to college. Take a look at you and then take a look at me."

Val faced him, her chin out. "Stop saying that. It's a lie. The fact that my skin is lighter is not a reason for me to be smarter than you. Skin and brains have *nothing* to do with each other."

Theresa crossed her fingers. She did not want them to talk about skin color. But silently she agreed with Tony. Wasn't Val the lightest one in the room? And Val always had had the highest marks. Wasn't she, Theresa, the darkest one here? And she always had had poor grades.

Cookie was running from one to another pointing and reciting, "You're a little black so you're a little dumb." When she came to Theresa, she chanted, "You're a lot black so you're a lot dumb."

"Shh!" Mrs. Gardiner snapped as if Cookie had said a curse word. The slap Cookie got made the Gardiner children laugh.

Theresa laughed, too. But she did not think Mrs. Gardiner was being hard on Cookie. Cookie's remark had hurt. This was not the first time Theresa wished she had been born with fairer skin.

Val hugged Theresa. "Don't feel bad, Tweedy. Cookie is a lot dumb because she doesn't know what's true and what's a lie white folks told us."

"That child is going right to bed," Mrs. Gardiner said. "All this talk is not going to get our work done."

Suddenly everyone remembered he had homework to do. Theresa and Laura sat on Val's single bed and studied spelling. She hoped Val would say more about brains and color not going together. She wished that Val were her sister, so that she could talk to her more often.

But there was no more talk. Soon it was bedtime. Mrs. Gardiner suggested that Theresa and Laura sleep at the head of the bed and Cookie at the foot.

"I don't want Tweedy to sleep in our bed. There's no room for her," Cookie cried before her mother could hush her up.

Theresa got out of her clothes and into pajamas. She tried not to mind Cookie's protest. She got into bed and Laura cuddled close.

"Don't mind Cookie," Laura whispered. "I love having you visit us."

"When my mother comes home, maybe you and I can sleep this way in my bed. My mother won't mind sleeping at the foot of the bed," Theresa said softly. She thought about her mother until at last she fell into a dreamless sleep.

Two days passed slowly. Theresa went to the hospital each day. Her mother was in an oxygen tent and seemed to be fast asleep all the time. She was on the critical list.

On Friday, Mrs. Gardiner went with her. Mrs. Gardiner's face was grave when she talked to the doctor. The doctor asked Theresa if she had any relatives who could take care of her if anything should happen to her mother.

"Don't let anything happen to my mother," Theresa begged. "I have nobody, and she has nobody. We take care of each other."

That night Mrs. Gardiner held Theresa on her lap after the others were in bed. "Poor baby," she crooned and rocked slowly back and forth. At exactly two o'clock in the morning a policeman came to tell them that Mrs. Ellmsby had died. Someone had to come with him to the hospital to get her clothes and sign certain papers. Mrs. Gardiner helped Theresa dress. She slipped Laura's coat on Theresa and held her hand as together they went with the policeman to the hospital.

The next few hours remained forever a blur in Theresa's memory. She could not believe that her mother would never again see her, call her name, tell her it was time for school. She could not believe that her mother would not be there to greet her after school. Nurses and doctors talked to her. Everyone was kind. Even the policeman patted her hand.

But no one eased the emptiness. She carried her mother's robe and slippers home in a paper bag. She wondered why.

The policeman said as he left them at their door, "A social worker will come to see you today." He smiled to Theresa and assured her that she had nothing to worry about. "You'll be well taken care of," he said before he bade them good night and went down the stairs.

Theresa did not care who came to see her. Or when. Her mother was dead. Nothing else mattered. In the morning, when the rest of the children quietly went off to school, Theresa sat numbly on the bed. She did not wonder what was to become of her. All she thought about was that now she was alone in the world. Really alone.

At Mrs. Gardiner's request, she went upstairs to get a change of underwear. In the apartment she walked from chair to chair. The coffeepot and the empty cups stood where she had left them.

"Ma," she said before she could stop herself. She had wanted to tell her mother that she would wash the dishes. But her mother was gone.

Carefully, Theresa washed and dried the dishes. She set them in their places, then took up a cloth and began to dust. She came to the ivy plant.

"Did you die, too?" Theresa touched the dried leaves. Footsteps were approaching the door. Theresa wiped her tears away quickly.

There was a tap on the door. A pleasant female voice asked, "May I come in?"

The woman explained that she was the social worker and that Mrs. Gardiner was waiting for them. She suggested that Theresa come downstairs with her.

"Take the ivy with you," the social worker said.

It did not seem worth the effort. The plant looked dead, but Theresa could not put it down. She brought it into the Gardiner apartment and set it on the kitchen window sill.

The social worker asked many questions about the Ellmsbys. Theresa knew only that everyone in her family was dead. She stood close to Mrs. Gardiner all the time the social worker was there.

After all the questions had been answered, Mrs. Gardiner said she would keep Theresa for a week or two. For that short time it would be possible to squeeze an extra person into the household.

"I'd keep you longer," Mrs. Gardiner explained, "but you know how crowded we are and how hard it is for me to keep up with the six I already have."

Theresa did know, yet it was not easy to think that soon she would be with strangers. She had somehow hoped that she might stay on with the Gardiners forever.

The social worker made plans to sell the Ellmsby furniture to pay the landlord what was due him. "We will also arrange for a small funeral," she promised.

She bent close to Theresa. "I'm going to try to find a private agency to take care of you, Theresa. Perhaps they will be able to find a good foster home for you."

"What will happen if they can't find a foster home?" Mrs. Gardiner asked.

"Then she will be placed in a children's shelter," the social worker answered. She added that in all probability Theresa would end up there. "Older Negro children are difficult to place," she said sadly. "Even babies have little chance for foster parents."

Theresa wiped her eyes before the tears could run down her face. She tried not to listen any more. No one could help her. She was alone and no one would want a dark-colored girl. She wished she could creep into some dark, dark place and never come out again.

Theresa did not lift her head until the social worker left. Then she went into the bathroom and shut the door behind her. "Isn't it bad enough to be an orphan?" she sobbed. "Do I have to be black, too?"

During the next few days Theresa thought a lot about being black, but she did not talk about it. She was afraid of being teased. Then on Monday, a social worker came from a private agency.

Miss Wilner was a huge white woman and even Theresa, sad as she was, had to admit that Miss Wilner filled a room with friendliness.

She noticed everyone. Cookie had a lovely ,mile; Laura had graceful hands; the twins were witty; and Val was just the right height and shape for a woman. And not one of the compliments was untrue.

About Theresa, Miss Wilner was equally honest. "Child, you look as skinny and tired as that poor bit of ivy on the window sill. Some loving care would do you both a world of good."

With her finger, the social worker poked the soil in the flowerpot. The soil scattered and some fell on the floor.

"Whoops!" Miss Wilner cried. "That's me all the time. I'm so big that I have to be careful with coffee cups and small flowerpots. I'm going to have to make up to that poor bit of ivy for my carelessness."

She puckered her nose. "I know what I'm going to do. I'm going to find that ivy a good home. Would you like to go with your plant if I can find such a place?"

"Nobody will want us," Theresa mumbled. "And even if you found us a place . . . we're not going to look any better."

Miss Wilner took Theresa's face in her hands. "Theresa, I hope I can find a good home for you. I'd like to prove to you how different *you* and your plant could look if you were given the chance."

Before she went to bed that night, Theresa spent a

long time looking at her plant. Would this tangled vine and these dried-out leaves again become the pretty plant it had been when she bought it for her mother?

That seemed as much of an impossibility as making her pretty. "Idle talk," she said to herself as she wearily got out of her clothes and went to bed.

Three

The weeks passed. Theresa stopped looking up at the fifth-floor windows. The apartment had been rented to another family, and seeing anyone at the familiar window made her cry.

She cried a lot. When anyone said "Mama," she could not control her tears. Tony warned her not to hover over her plant so much. "You'll drown it the way you're going," he said with mischief in his eyes.

She was crying the day Miss Wilner came to tell her that a temporary home had been found for her. She cried all during the time Miss Wilner told Val and Mrs. Gardiner the story. Theresa barely heard when Miss Wilner said that it was only to be temporary.

After she heard that, she didn't listen any more. Miss Wilner told Mrs. Gardiner that the Chintons, Theresa's new foster parents, lived just outside of the city, on Long Island, near Jamaica, Queens. They had a two-bedroom apartment in a cooperative. Mrs. Chinton was not sure she liked living there, but while they were in that building they had an extra room and wanted a child to share their home.

Mr. Chinton worked right there and he liked the building development. These two factors were important enough to keep Mrs. Chinton settled for a while. So although the placement might be temporary, it was possible that it might turn out to be permanent.

When she had finished the story, Miss Wilner smiled at Theresa. "And I didn't forget your ivy, either. Mr. Chinton is a first-class gardener. I talked to him about your plant and he said he would take care of it."

By this time the rest of the family had crowded into the kitchen. Bethina thought living in Jamaica was "super." Benjy thought having any kind of a room to himself was the "greatest."

Tony hushed everyone. He knew about families that made a living out of keeping foster children. "Do the Chintons have other foster children?" His eyes narrowed as they met Miss Wilner's.

Theresa stopped crying. She, too, had heard stories about foster homes. How could she have forgotten? Her heart thudded against her ribs. She did not want to go. She ran into the bedroom and closed the door.

She did not hear Miss Wilner say, "Mr. Chinton

works in the post office that was built right inside the cooperative. Mrs. Chinton is home all day. That is one of the reasons they want a child. She is lonely. All the years while they were helping put their boys through college, she worked in a slipcover factory. Now the boys are away in graduate school and she isn't used to being home with no responsibilities."

Miss Wilner looked around. "Where's Theresa?" she asked. She went into the bedroom and put her arms around Theresa's trembling shoulders. "You'll like Mrs. Chinton. She does beautiful sewing. She was pleased when I told her you had helped your mother with her sewing."

I guess I have to expect something like this, she thought. *A black girl is lucky if she gets any kind of foster home.* She glanced up at Miss Wilner suspiciously. This woman was acting as if she were giving Theresa a party.

Theresa lowered her eyes before Miss Wilner could see them. She did not want anyone to think she was afraid of sewing for anyone. *Under all those fine words,* she thought, *this white woman is telling me I'm going to live with a janitor and his wife.* She knew from experience that most janitors took care of any flower boxes or grass that grew around their buildings. She also knew that janitors' wives often did cleaning and other work for the tenants. She pictured herself wielding the big mop she had seen the janitor use on their halls and staircases.

Miss Wilner coaxed her into the kitchen. Val grinned encouragingly at Theresa. "Tweedy, don't you want to hear about the boys? There are two of them. Away at school. Maybe you'll introduce me to them."

Theresa nodded. "I guess," she said glumly. She knew that Val wanted to show her the bright side of the move.

Miss Wilner asked Theresa to put on a coat and come out for a walk. Theresa said she did not have a coat and did not feel much like walking.

"We can't talk in here," Miss Wilner said cheerfully. She raised her brows, then reached into her pocketbook and fished out a bag of chocolate kisses. She tossed them to Benjy.

"These will do you more good than they'll do me. Will you hand these out and find a way to keep everyone quiet in the bedroom so that Theresa, your mother, and I can hear ourselves talk?"

Benjy thought he could and with Val's help he cleared the kitchen.

When the room was quiet, Miss Wilner and Mrs. Gardiner made a list of clothes that had to be bought, starting with a coat and sweater. Theresa wondered numbly what good new clothes were to a scrub girl, a janitor's helper.

The list completed, Miss Wilner asked about Theresa's school. There were books to return and a transfer to get. The social worker asked Theresa how she did in school. Theresa frowned.

She was two years behind in reading. Her mother had promised to get her a tutor as soon as she went back to work. To make Theresa feel better, Mrs. Gardiner talked about her own children. Except for Val, all the Gardiner children were poor readers. Mrs. Gardiner blamed their backwardness on the teachers. She claimed that in an all-Negro school, the teachers did not teach because they were prejudiced and did not truly believe that black children were able to learn like white children.

Tony stuck his head out of the bedroom door and said that his mother spoke the truth. He had begun school uptown in a class that was mostly white. He had been doing well. Then the family had moved to Harlem when his father could not find a job.

"And look at me now, an about-to-be dropout . . ."

Val pulled him back into the bedroom, but he stuck his head outside the door again.

"But anyhow, here in Harlem we're all black. Maybe that's what's needed."

Mrs. Gardiner went on to talk about her husband. She said she hoped Tony and Benjy would not have trouble getting jobs. Each job her husband had gotten was worse than the one he had lost. Finally, he lost all hope of getting a good job here and moved to another city. Now she was alone with the children.

"Down here in Harlem I can tell you," she ended sadly, "the teachers don't think the children can learn so they don't teach them. Copying from the board is what they do most of the day. Show us your fingers, Tweedy."

Theresa let Mrs. Gardiner hold up her writing fingers. They were calloused from holding a pencil. Miss Wilner sniffed. Theresa did not like Miss Wilner when she did that.

Miss Wilner took Theresa's hand in hers. "I guess some of what you say is true, Mrs. Gardiner. But the problem is more complicated than that." She looked at Theresa seriously yet warmly.

"I think that being born a Negro in this country does something harmful to a child. He feels inferior, and because he feels that way he can't work as well as the child who feels good about himself." Mrs. Gardiner nodded vigorously.

"A lot has to be done," Miss Wilner continued. "If only Dr. King were alive to lead us peacefully into integration. I know that if people work together and learn to live together everyone will benefit."

"You can say that again, Miss Wilner," Val called from the bedroom. "Dr. King's great. I heard him on a record once."

Tony snorted. "You're all wet. We got to work this out alone. If it means riots, at least we're doing something for ourselves."

"Mind your tongue," Mrs. Gardiner warned him.

"She started it," Tony retorted, pointing at Val.

Mrs. Gardiner got up and started toward the bedroom.

Miss Wilner stopped her. "Let them talk," she said. "I think rioting is dangerous, but I can understand how frustrated people can feel when nothing good happens."

She doesn't understand, Theresa thought sadly. *She can't because she's white.* But she was too frightened by all the talk of black and white to say anything at all.

Miss Wilner shook hands with Tony and with the

other Gardiners. To Mrs. Gardiner she said, "You've done a fine job with your family. They speak up about their own thoughts."

"See you tomorrow at nine," she said to Theresa as she picked up her portfolio and handbag.

Theresa did not take her hands from her face. Miss Wilner patted her on the head. "I know how you feel, honey. But things will be better tomorrow."

Mrs. Gardiner went out the door with the social worker and the two stood outside talking. Tony came to the table and pulled Theresa's hands away from her face.

"Did you ask if you get an allowance?"

"Tony, stop pestering Tweedy," Val yelled.

"Did you ask if you could have visitors? Or if you could come here?" Tony held her so that she had to look at him.

"Tony, you're scaring her," Val cried.

"I'm not. I'm being practical," he answered.

"You have no sense," Val said distinctly. "Think of Tweedy. She has to go live with that family, and it sounds fine to me."

"I *am* thinking of Tweedy," Tony retorted. "What do you say, kid, am I thinking of you? Do you want to go there?"

Theresa could not answer. Mrs. Gardiner could not keep her—that was clear. To remain here where there was no room for her was impossible. Yet she did not want to go to that other home.

Tony's eyes searched hers. She could not admit that she wanted to stay where she was not wanted. That would sound as if she were ungrateful.

"Mama," she wailed as she ran to the window sill where her plant stood. "Mama, what should I do?"

She cradled the plant in her arms, dashed past Tony and the twins, ducked as she passed Mrs. Gardiner's and Miss Wilner's outstretched hands, and ran down the stairs.

"Looking for me?" Miss Wilner called.

"I'm looking for nobody," Theresa sobbed. "Me and my plant are going away forever."

Miss Wilner stopped Tony and Benjy. "I'll get her," she said as she started down the steps faster than it seemed possible for such a heavy woman.

"Theresa, stop," Miss Wilner begged.

Theresa ran ahead, almost tumbling down the last few steps.

The building door was open, and a strong wind was blowing into the hallway. Miss Wilner kept calling down to Theresa. She was only a few steps behind.

Down into her hiding place Theresa crept. Her hands cradled her plant to keep the wind away. She shut her eyes to keep even the little bit of light out. She wanted nothing but darkness and silence.

"Tweedy."

Miss Wilner's voice was barely audible. "Tweedy, please come out." There was a pause. Then the social worker said plaintively, "I'm too fat to crawl in there with you and I do want to talk to you."

Theresa did not answer. What was there to talk about?

"That plant will catch a cold," Miss Wilner said.

Theresa curled her arms tighter around the flowerpot. The pot was getting colder by the second. The draft from the door was blowing through the vines and making them tremble.

Miss Wilner was whispering. "Remember what I told you upstairs about my being too fat? I don't think a person ought to accept everything life dishes out, and I wish I were more of a fighter than an accepter. Then I would eat less. Maybe then I could crawl in there next to you . . . where I would like to be."

Theresa grunted with displeasure. This white woman talked too much. She wished Miss Wilner were thousands of miles away.

"I know how you feel," Miss Wilner said.

"You do not!" Theresa cried out. She opened her eyes.

"Then *tell* me how you feel," Miss Wilner answered.

The social worker's voice was kind. The hand she had stuck out toward Theresa beckoned Theresa closer. Accidentally Theresa's arm touched the hand. Despite its size it was gentle. Its warmth felt good. She began to whimper.

"I don't want to go to a foster home and I can't stay here," Theresa said after she got control of her tears. "Nobody wants a black girl . . . a dark one . . . I wish I were dead like my mother."

Miss Wilner's hand firmly pulled her out of the corner. "The Chintons want you. They want you very much."

"Are you sure?" Theresa asked. Even if it weren't true it would be nice to hear the words.

She sighed with relief when Miss Wilner replied,

"I'm very sure. I talked to them and told them about you. And Mr. Dyson, my boss, talked to them, too. I can't guarantee that you will like it right away. Remember, a new home takes getting used to. You will need to get used to the way Mr. and Mrs. Chinton do things, and they in turn will have to get used to having a girl around instead of boys."

Theresa thought for a minute. "Are they dark like me . . . ?"

Miss Wilner pulled her all the way out from under the steps. "Yes, Theresa, I'm sure of that, too. What I'm not sure of is why you run away instead of standing still and talking up for yourself."

She sat down on the steps with Theresa. Every time someone came up the stairs. Theresa had to get up to let them pass. Theresa saw their curious glances as they went by. But she did not care what anyone thought. Nothing mattered now. Orphans had no choice.

Miss Wilner was telling her a story about a kitten she had gotten from a friend in the country. The kitten hated staying in the house, yet whenever Miss Wilner let her go out into the back yard, the kitten came back into the house terrified. Once it was a dog, a tiny dog from next door, that had frightened the kitten. The next time it was a fire engine clanging by. The third time it was a girl who came up to the kitten and tried to pick her up.

The story held Theresa's attention. Miss Wilner told it with sadness and excitement. "I finally decided that I either had to cure my kitten or send it back to the country," Miss Wilner said. "This was one time I could not accept a situation. My kitten and I were both becoming nervous wrecks."

"What did you do?" Theresa hoped Miss Wilner had not sent the kitten back to the country.

"What would you have done?"

Theresa thought. "It was only noises scaring the kitten. I'd take her out and show her what made the noises . . ." she said slowly.

Miss Wilner chuckled. "Exactly what I did. I held the kitten in my arms and let her smell the puppy and the girl. She soon got used to dogs and children and later forgot to mind the sirens. She's a big happy cat, now."

The social worker got up and stretched. "Time to go up now. What did you think of my story?"

"It was okay," Theresa answered. She stood up, too.

Miss Wilner began walking up the stairs. "Can you guess why I remembered it today?"

Theresa was one step behind her. "Because I ran away?" she asked.

Miss Wilner turned and looked down at her. "Do you think my kitten was a coward?"

"No," Theresa replied. "She didn't know about dogs and children. You had to teach her."

"Can I take you in my arms and teach you what you'll need to know in your new home?"

Theresa stood silently on the step. Several children she knew by name bounded past her.

"Friends of yours?" Miss Wilner asked.

Theresa shook her head. "Only Laura's my friend."

"How come a nice girl like you has only one friend?"

Miss Wilner was puffing noisily as she rested on the first-floor landing. When she caught her breath she said, "I'll bet you would have lots of friends if you gave kids a chance to know you."

"Who cares about friends." Theresa did not move until the social worker did. The social worker's eyes were soft and the hand she was holding out was gentle.

"Want to make a bargain?"

"What kind?" Theresa asked shyly.

"One to help the both of us. It'll help me get up stairs easier and it will help you make friends with your new family easier."

"I don't need friends," Theresa said sadly.

"You need friends as much as I need to lose weight," Miss Wilner replied gravely. "This is the bargain. I never can stay on a diet when I'm worried. Now I'm going to promise you that I'll keep my diet and you promise me that you will try not to run away when you get scared."

Miss Wilner had her hand out. "What do you say? Is it a bargain?" She waited for Theresa to answer. "For my sake, will you shake on it?"

"If it will help you"—Theresa put her hand in the big one—"I'll promise."

Four

All the Gardiners helped Theresa get ready for meeting her foster parents. Val washed her hair and straightened it with a hot comb so that it lay straight on her shoulders. Afterwards she rolled the strands on thick curlers so that it could be combed out into a soft flip.

Cookie held the curlers and pins. Laura held the mirror. Tony polished Theresa's shoes until the scuffs were covered. Bethina and Benjy cut out cardboard soles to put inside the shoes to hide the holes in the bottoms. Mrs. Gardiner washed Theresa's blouse. It would be dry enough to iron by morning.

That night Theresa held on to Laura's hand. Laura

brushed a finger under Theresa's eyes. "I thought you were crying . . . you're so quiet."

Theresa almost cried then. *Who would worry about her tomorrow? Tomorrow and the days after that . . . Who would care if she were quiet?*

Laura cuddled close. "Val says Jamaica is not too far away from here. The subway goes there, and we can write letters. Did you ever get a letter? I didn't."

Cookie crawled up to the head of the bed. She wanted to know what a foster home was, why Theresa was going to one, and could she and Laura go, too, and have a room to themselves.

Theresa pressed her close. "I wish I had a family with brothers and sisters. The way you have. I'd rather have that than have a room to myself."

"Why?" Cookie asked.

Laura pushed Cookie down to her place on the bed. "It'd take a year to tell you that. Shut up and go to sleep."

That night Theresa dreamed that she ran away and hid in some dark, safe place. Only no one came to find her. The darkness began to press down on her eyes until it hurt.

She awoke crying, "Laura, you better come with me. I'm scared to go alone."

Mrs. Gardiner came in and patted Theresa's hand. It was time for everyone to get up. Val took time out from her own dressing to comb out Theresa's hair. Tony went back and forth from his room to the girls' room, fussing about the cardboard soles.

When no one was looking he whispered to Theresa,

"Tweedy, you talk up for yourself with those agency people. Make them get you some warm clothes. Miss Wilner will talk up, but you have to help her by talking up, too."

"Better eat today," Mrs. Gardiner said as she prepared a bowl of oatmeal for Theresa. "Nothing like food in the stomach to keep the heart singing."

When it was time for school, Mrs. Gardiner shooed the children out one by one. "Tweedy isn't going away forever. Off with you." One hug and kiss was all she allowed, even to Laura. "You girls can write to each other all you like. That'll do you both more good than all this smooching. Now off to school with you or you'll have Tweedy crying again."

The house was terribly still after everyone had gone to school. It was like the day after her mother had died. She was not sorry when nine o'clock brought Miss Wilner to the door.

Theresa was wearing one of Bethina's sweaters until she got her own. First, they were to stop by the school to get Theresa a transfer. Later they were to go to the agency for a medical examination and to meet Mr. Dyson. He would give them a check, and then they would go shopping.

"All of this has to be done before four o'clock, when the rush hour starts," Miss Wilner explained. "I hate to drive in heavy traffic."

Theresa walked behind the big woman. The four flights of stairs seemed shorter than usual. The outside door seemed to have moved right up to the bottom step.

Miss Wilner took Theresa's arm. "I know this is hard.

But I'll be with you all day. By five o'clock you will be in your new home. Perhaps you can telephone and say good night to the Gardiners."

"They have no phone."

"Then write to them tonight. I'll leave a stamped, addressed envelope for you."

"I have nothing to write about."

Miss Wilner cheerfully replied, "That's because you have never done things without them before. Laura will love to hear about the things you see and do. And you'll want to know what she's doing."

They walked out of the building. The sun was cutting the street into light and dark patches. Theresa turned her head so that she could see only the shadows.

"Think I can make it?" Miss Wilner asked as she stopped in front of a small red car.

In spite of herself, Theresa had to giggle. The big woman was pretending she could not get behind the wheel. She stood away and looked at herself, then with her hands she measured the space between the seat and the wheel.

"I'll have to lose two inches before I can get in there," she said. "That is, if I want to get in there comfortably. Today I begin working on my diet. My new motto is— *more fight, eat right.*"

She opened the door and Theresa got into the car. Miss Wilner laughed. "It's bigger than you thought it was, isn't it?" She came around and slid into the driver's seat. "Troubles are that way. Some of them seem bigger than they turn out to be."

All the way to the school she kept asking Theresa

questions about the kinds of clothes she liked, and hair styles and movies.

Getting a transfer took only a short time. The principal and the secretary were friendly and helpful.

"Now, that didn't hurt, did it?" Miss Wilner asked. "The rest will be just as painless."

The agency turned out to be nothing but a building. Theresa had not known what to expect, but she had not expected to find the agency to be anything as ordinary as a building.

They came to a small office where they saw a man behind a desk. For a moment the man seemed to be white. Theresa was introduced to him. He took her hand and pressed it. The way his eyes met hers was the way Tony's did—direct and searching.

Theresa gulped. This man was not white. He was a Negro! "Mr. Dyson?" she asked Miss Wilner. "Is this your boss?" When Miss Wilner laughed and said yes, Theresa gulped again. In all her life she had never seen or heard of a black man being the boss of a white person.

She thought fast. She had heard of Negroes who pretended to be white in order to get good jobs. Mr. Dyson must have done that and that was why he was here. She glanced at Miss Wilner to see if she had given Mr. Dyson's act away.

Miss Wilner was beaming at her with an encouraging smile. Theresa slid back in her chair and listened to the questions being asked. She wanted to do her best for Mr. Dyson, who probably needed the job very much to do such a dangerous thing.

She found talking to Mr. Dyson easy. He asked if

she was frightened about going to a foster home that might be only temporary. She assured him that she did not care about that.

Mr. Dyson grinned. "Smart girl," he said. "If the Chintons move, or decide for whatever reason that they can't keep you, you can always be sure that the agency will take care of you. You will never be alone again. Someone from our agency will always be available."

The way he said that made Theresa's eyes grow wet. He seemed to mean every word. And the way he talked about the clothes she would need also seemed to show he cared.

She wondered why they spent so much time deciding whether to get her two skirts and two pairs of jeans or one dress and one skirt with the jeans. Since she expected to be mopping floors, she would need more jeans and no dresses.

Miss Wilner said that Mrs. Chinton might want to make a dress with Theresa, since they both enjoyed sewing. Theresa immediately said, "Making clothes is cheaper. I think it's better if I make the dress, if I need one."

From the way Mr. Dyson talked, Theresa began to think that Mrs. Chinton did more sewing than cleaning. Perhaps Mr. Chinton had only a little bit of gardening to do and had plenty of time to take care of the building.

To herself she mumbled, "I'm glad. I'd rather sew than do the janitor work."

An hour later she was in the street again. She had been examined by a doctor and a dentist. Miss Wilner had the check and they were ready for shopping.

"Lunch, first," Miss Wilner said.

Theresa could not force herself to eat the sandwich Miss Wilner bought for her. Miss Wilner picked at her salad. "I said I'm beginning my diet today. Usually when I'm nervous I eat double what I need. I wish I were like you."

"I can't eat when I'm worried. But why are you worried?" Theresa asked curiously.

"Think it isn't nerve wracking to fix up families?" Miss Wilner demanded. She spooned all her dessert into her mouth and swallowed it before she continued. "I like to match children up with parents. Now I think you and the Chintons ought to do well together. You like the same things, look somewhat alike. You've never had brothers and must always have wanted some just as they must have always wanted a sister."

Theresa admitted that she had always envied her friends' big families. Miss Wilner paid for their lunch and waited until they were seated in the car before she went on.

"I want to make sure everything goes right—and to make sure that you know what is expected of you. I've already met with the Chintons and told them what they might expect from you."

"They'll expect me to help them and obey," Theresa said without a quiver in her voice.

"Right," Miss Wilner boomed. "And now that you have thought of that, have you thought about what you will call them?" She pulled out of the parking space and into the stream of traffic. "You'll have to call them something, you know."

"What do other kids call them . . . foster parents, that is?"

"Oh," Miss Wilner said. "Some call them Aunt and Uncle and some call them Mother and Dad, or Mom and Pop."

"Mama!" Theresa exclaimed. "I couldn't call anybody that."

"What did you call your mother?" Miss Wilner asked. "I call my mother just that. Mother."

"Do you have a mother?" Theresa asked. She did not think of grown-ups as having mothers. Miss Wilner assured her that she had one and that she had always called her Mother.

Theresa thought that Miss Wilner's mother would be very old. "Where does your mother live?" she asked the social worker.

Miss Wilner answered and then said, "You could call them Mr. and Mrs. Chinton, but I would not like to be called that by a foster child. Yet it's up to you—"

Theresa was glad when Miss Wilner changed the subject from names. Her eyes were smarting with held-back tears. Little as she liked talking about school, she preferred that to thinking about calling anyone Mother.

Miss Wilner thought Theresa might be glad to know that Mrs. Chinton had promised to do a lot of school-work with Theresa. She had helped the boys when they needed help in the lower grades. When the boys went on to high school, she had enrolled in night school and had managed to keep up with them until they went to college.

Theresa mumbled, "I'd rather do the sewing. I hate

reading. I never get it right."

Miss Wilner laughed joyously. "I'll bet you won't be saying that next year. It has never failed. No sooner does a kid begin getting good marks, when suddenly he falls in love with school. His teacher becomes bearable, too."

"I'll never like school . . ."

"You'll like this one. It's new and pretty."

"Who cares about pretty. I won't know a single person."

"You'll make friends quickly. I know you will," Miss Wilner said. "That's why I want you to pick out pretty clothes."

"It won't make any difference. Clothes don't change people. Nobody'll like me . . ."

Miss Wilner pulled up to the curb in front of a large department store. "Laura liked you."

Theresa dug her nails into her fingertips. She said that Laura had been her only friend.

Miss Wilner turned to Theresa and said seriously, "Making friends is a two-way deal. If you look and act stand-offish, kids think you don't like them. They don't want their feelings hurt, so they go elsewhere to make friends."

Theresa wondered if she had ever acted stand-offish. She remembered the times she had refused to go to the park, or to jump rope. As she went into the store with the social worker, she told herself, "I wasn't stand-offish. I had to help my mother sew . . ." Had the girls thought her uppity?

There was no time to ask herself any more questions.

Miss Wilner and a saleslady were bringing out clothes—underthings, of all types and colors.

"I don't care which you buy," Theresa answered listlessly.

"You must pick something or we'll be here all day," Miss Wilner said. She finally eliminated all but two slips. Then she said, "Theresa, I don't care how you decide, but you must choose one of these slips."

Without opening her eyes Theresa picked one. That was what happened at every counter. Miss Wilner bought two of each item that Theresa picked.

Piled high with boxes, she followed Miss Wilner, who was equally loaded with boxes, out to the car. She heard a child say as she passed, "Mommy, isn't that girl lucky to get so many new things?"

But Theresa did not feel lucky at all. She let Miss Wilner shut the car door and wished she had the nerve to run away—forever and ever.

The car started. Miss Wilner asked, "Weren't we both going to try to act differently when things looked bad?"

"I'm not running away," Theresa answered guiltily. How had Miss Wilner guessed her thoughts?

"That's true, but you're making up your mind not to like or trust the Chintons. Why don't you wait until you meet them at least?"

Miss Wilner sounded as if she were disappointed in Theresa. To defend herself, Theresa pointed out that the social worker had not kept her promise either. "You ate dessert and that's not on a weight-losing diet," Theresa exclaimed. She had seen Mrs. Gardiner eat and Mrs. Gardiner was on a perpetual diet.

A smile was Theresa's answer. Miss Wilner giggled. "You're right. I had only fruit but I should not have had even that. I'm going to have to do better than that —even when I'm nervous."

"I'll try to like the Chintons . . ."

"And will you wait until you get into your new class before you decide no one will like you?"

Theresa grinned shyly. "Do you think I can change enough so they will like me?"

"Maybe you won't need to change. Why don't you wait and see," Miss Wilner answered as the car once again moved into traffic.

Theresa thought about that as they drove up to the Gardiner's building, so that Theresa could return Bethina's sweater and pick up her old things.

Five

Theresa's parting from the Gardiners was brief. While Miss Wilner waited below, she ran upstairs, hugged and kissed each of the six Gardiners, took the paper bag with her clothes, thanked Bethina for the use of her sweater, and stood in the doorway with tears in her eyes.

Mrs. Gardiner put her plant in her free hand. "We'll see you soon. And remember, you write to us."

Theresa nodded. She felt the tears beginning to roll down her face. Before they came, she raised her hand with the paper bag in it and forced a little smile to her lips.

"Good-by," she said and, clutching her plant against her trembling body, she ran down the stairs.

In the car she watched the Harlem streets roll by with melancholy slowness. She looked out of the window as if she were saying good-by to everything forever.

At each corner a traffic light. Each light a wait. And each wait gave her a little more time to look at the familiar stores, the solid rows of houses, the tired-looking young men lounging on the stoops. Even the overflowing garbage cans lining the sides of the buildings looked beautiful as she passed them.

Miss Wilner said nothing. She whistled a sad little tune until they had passed the last light on the last street in Harlem.

"The Triborough Bridge," Miss Wilner announced as she reached into her purse for money. She paid the toll and smiled.

"Sorry to be leaving Harlem?" she asked sympathetically.

Theresa looked up and saw Miss Wilner's gentle smile. Miss Wilner said, "I didn't think anyone could regret leaving such a dirty, ugly section of the city."

"It's not ugly," Theresa answered. "I always lived here."

"You'll like Queens."

"I'll hate it," Theresa whispered. "I won't know anyone. I won't know any place . . ."

Miss Wilner chuckled. "Remember. We are going to wait and see before we make up our minds that things are hopeless. Right?"

With an effort, she tried to show interest when the

social worker pointed to the left and said, "That's the airport. See the planes coming in." She tried to watch the boats on the river, the buildings, and the cars. After what seemed hours, the car turned off the parkway. Once again she saw city streets. On one of them Theresa saw a gaily painted store window with a sign AFRICAN METHODIST CHURCH. Just like in Harlem!

She sat up. The church she and her mother had gone to was like this one. Would she see other things that reminded her of Harlem?

They turned a corner. On one side of the street she saw a park with a lake and a playground. Benches were set under many trees.

"Is this where the Chintons live?" Theresa asked hopefully. If Mr. Chinton was a gardener he might live near a park.

"Not quite," Miss Wilner answered. She explained that the cooperative was several blocks away. They were riding along the boulevard that separated the cooperative from the rest of the neighborhood. All the small houses they were passing belonged to Negroes or were rented by them. Until the cooperative had been built, this neighborhood, like Harlem, had been a ghetto.

Theresa did not have to know what ghetto meant to know that only black people lived in these houses. She thought for a moment and decided that only white people lived in the cooperative. In Manhattan there were streets which had only Negro people and right across those streets were houses where only whites lived.

This place is not so different from Harlem after all, Theresa said to herself, as Miss Wilner drove into a street that was shaped like a circle.

"Isn't this pretty?" Miss Wilner asked. Facing them was a group of four houses shaped like an E. Each house made two fourteen-story E's back to back.

Miss Wilner found a parking space. "This is a huge development," she said. "There are five circles like this. Each circle has four buildings, and each building has three separate wings with three banks of elevators. They have their own shopping center called a mall and there's a community building. Tremendous, isn't it?"

Theresa looked around. In the center of the circle was a garden full of flowers. Around the buildings was lots of grass. To the left of the fourth building was an enormous empty lot. From the size of that lot and from the size of the grassy areas, it was clear that many gardeners had been at work.

The flower garden itself must take many hours to care for. No wonder they need me, Theresa thought as she got out of the car. She took firm hold of her plant and her bag full of clothes.

"Help with some of the boxes," Miss Wilner said cheerfully.

Theresa tucked a box under each arm and juggled her plant and bagful of clothes so that she would not drop them. It seemed silly to be carrying all these new clothes to a place where most of the time would be spent working. All she would need in this place was jeans and more jeans. No one gardened in skirts and blouses. She stumbled and Miss Wilner caught her. "Scared?" Miss Wilner asked.

Theresa met her eyes steadily. She did not want to

seem scared of work. "I guess they do need me," she said as loudly as she could make herself talk.

All of a sudden Theresa began to be aware of the women and the baby carriages coming along the paths. They were all white. No mistaking them. Her knees felt wobbly. She had never been among so many white people at one time. She was almost afraid to look around. She hoped Miss Wilner would not ask her another question until they were away from all these white people.

Theresa juggled the packages and her plant to keep them from falling while she followed Miss Wilner into the fourth building. Theresa kept far to the right so that she would not brush against a white man walking with a small boy.

In the large tiled hallway she searched for the steps leading down into the basement, or a door marked JANITOR.

"This way," Miss Wilner called. "Middle section, odd elevator. The building sections are separate from each other and the elevators stop every other floor."

A white woman rode up in the elevator with them. Theresa politely stepped to the rear of the car. Mrs. Chinton must be working for one of the tenants in the building, Theresa decided. She would not be through until five o'clock.

She glanced at Miss Wilner's wrist watch. Four thirty. She had not known how tired she was until she had seen the time. *How will I ever last until Mrs. Chinton is finished working and takes me to her house?* she wondered.

Or, would she be expected to get right to work? She

took a deep breath and said very softly, "I'll do anything I'm told to do. I promised to try things out before I say I can't."

Miss Wilner rang a bell and at once the door opened. A short, dark-skinned woman with short, fuzzy hair said, "Come in. Come in and let me help you."

Theresa warmed to this woman. Her mother had often wished she had the courage to wear her hair natural. Lots of women in Harlem wore their hair short these days. Theresa thought it took a lot of courage to go around looking like an African. She was glad her mother had taught her to straighten her hair at home with a hot comb. But she admired the few brave girls who dared to wear nappy hair to school. She said hello politely to Mrs. Chinton and wondered where the white lady who owned the apartment was.

Mrs. Chinton smiled. "Do come in, Theresa." She tried to take Theresa's packages from her.

Theresa grew embarrassed. "I'm sorry I stared," she murmured as she held on tightly to her plant and paper bag.

Miss Wilner put all of the packages on the couch where Mrs. Chinton had laid the first package. She took her coat off and urged Theresa to make herself comfortable.

Theresa watched Mrs. Chinton for some sign of disapproval. Certainly the lady of the house would not like to see Mrs. Chinton's guests making themselves at home in the living room.

There seemed to be no hurry. Mrs. Chinton was asking Miss Wilner if she had seen the view from the terrace. "Come see the house, Theresa," Mrs. Chinton said.

Miss Wilner said she had time and insisted that Theresa put her boxes on top of the others. "Don't you want to see the place?" Miss Wilner asked.

"I never saw this kind of apartment before," Theresa said softly. Mrs. Chinton put her hand lightly on Theresa's shoulder. Theresa said to herself, "Mrs. Chinton understands that I've never been in a white person's house before. She must be nice to take me through it before her lady comes back."

With her arms free of everything but the plant, Theresa looked around the room. It was larger than any she had been in. One side was all window. The terrace was out there. She held her breath while Mrs. Chinton opened the glass door and let her see the window boxes full of plants and flowers which lined the railings.

Slowly Theresa turned until she had seen everything: drapes the color of autumn leaves, a television set built into a wall full of shelves, books and plants everywhere, and a soft couch and two chairs facing each other to make talking easier.

"Wow!" Theresa exclaimed. "This is living."

Underfoot Theresa felt deep carpeting. She glanced down to see if accidentally she had brought dirt in on her shoes. What would the lady of the house say to Mrs. Chinton if she found marks on her yellow rug?

"Lucky I'm wearing my new shoes," Theresa whispered. "I didn't have time to dirty them yet."

Mrs. Chinton laughed. "Surprisingly enough, this rug is light but it does not show dirt, I'm glad to say. With

all the gardening going on here, I'd never get done cleaning otherwise."

She led Miss Wilner and Theresa down a narrow hall. They passed a pretty kitchen and dinette. They passed a small bathroom with a glass-enclosed tub.

"How do you like this, Theresa?" Mrs. Chinton asked as she ushered her into a blue-and-white bedroom. "Let me take that plant, now. And you can bring some of the packages in from the living room, Theresa."

Miss Wilner in her booming voice said, "Isn't this lovely, Theresa? Simply lovely!"

Theresa held on to her plant. Could anyone really live in a room as pretty as this? There was a couch with a blue-plaid bedspread. There was a desk and bookshelves painted the blue of the bedspread. On the window sill there were blue flowers in white pots. For a long moment Theresa stared at the carpeting. She did not want to go into this room. She and her plant in its small brown pot were out of place here. Surely the lady of the house would be furious at Mrs. Chinton for allowing strangers in.

"Take your coat off, Theresa," Mrs. Chinton coaxed. "I've done everything but find a place for these things the boys have outgrown," she said, pointing to a carton filled with skates of various kinds and balls. "Dad will do that when he comes up. Meanwhile take your coat off and bring your things in here."

"I'll wait outside until you're ready," Theresa said hesitantly.

"You don't think the room is ready enough for you?" Mrs. Chinton asked.

"Not the room. I mean . . . I'll wait until *you're* ready." Theresa told Mrs. Chinton with her eyes showing how frightened she was of being caught in this white person's house.

Mrs. Chinton looked away from Theresa and down at herself. Her housedress was starched crisply. Her collar lay flat and smooth.

"Me? You think I'm not ready?" Mrs. Chinton ran her hands over her hair.

Miss Wilner took the plant out of Theresa's hands and was about to unbutton Theresa's coat when Theresa moved toward the studio couch.

"I'll put this carton wherever you want it," Theresa cried helpfully.

"What's the hurry?" Miss Wilner asked. She looked puzzled.

"Those things aren't in the way," Mrs. Chinton said. "They are the boys' things that are too good to throw away."

"Oh, you want to get them out of here," Theresa said. "Mrs. Gardiner sometimes goes out to work in people's houses and they sometimes let her take things home for the kids. I guess *this* lady would rather throw them away than let you take them . . ."

"What are you talking about, Theresa?" Miss Wilner asked. Something in Miss Wilner's face made Theresa look up. The social worker's face was red.

"I'm sorry," Theresa murmured, not knowing what she had done. "I just wanted to get out of here before the lady of the house comes home. I don't want Mrs. Chinton to get in trouble because of me . . ." Theresa was too tired to hold back her tears. Miss Wilner and Mrs. Chinton were staring at her so strangely.

"Theresa," Miss Wilner said. "What lady? Of what house?"

Mrs. Chinton came close to Theresa. In Theresa's ear she said, "You think a white lady owns this apartment and that I clean house for her?"

Theresa sniffled. She began buttoning her coat, but Mrs. Chinton's arms were too tightly wound around her. "Child, I'm the one that lives in this apartment. Dad and I and now you. This is *your* room. Understand? We live here."

While the words sank in, Mrs. Chinton held Theresa close. "This room is for me?" Theresa finally gasped.

"Except on holidays when the boys come home," Mrs. Chinton answered. "You don't mind sleeping on the living-room couch for a week or two, do you?"

Miss Wilner laughed her big laugh. "This couch opens to sleep two. Now isn't it a shame to let a nice room like this go empty for months at a time?"

Mrs. Chinton helped Theresa off with her coat. Theresa was speechless. Miss Wilner looked at the pot of ivy she had taken from Theresa.

"Can we find a place for this?"

Theresa wanted to put the pot behind her back. Where in this room could she put this scraggly thing? She put out her hand and Miss Wilner gave her the plant.

In the mirror on the closet door, Theresa saw herself. *We look all wrong here,* she thought. She saw Mrs. Chinton in the mirror. Mrs. Chinton's eyes were shining. Tiny wrinkles danced under her eyes as she came toward Theresa.

"Is that the plant Miss Wilner told us about? Let me have it. We must find a special place for it because you will want to keep it forever. Let me put it on this shelf."

Theresa saw the little brown pot go toward the blue shelf. Her heart beat hard against her ribs. She dreaded seeing her plant near the others in this room. She wanted to snatch the plant out of Mrs. Chinton's hands. She wanted to run out of this apartment where things were unfamiliar and fancy.

Miss Wilner made a face that said, "Remember!" Theresa swallowed her fear and sat down on the edge of the chair near the desk.

"There, see the poor little thing," Mrs. Chinton said in her clear low voice. "It will like this shady spot. Look at it. It looks better already."

Theresa managed to say, "Thank you." The plant did look better with its vine draped around the pot instead of hanging loose. She looked around her at the drapes and at the furniture. *Maybe even I'll look better living in a home like this,* she thought. *Or maybe I'll wake up in some shelter and find out this was all a dream.*

Six

When Miss Wilner said it was time for her to leave, Theresa started to cry. Miss Wilner took her aside and said, "You must feel like Beauty did when her father left her in that beautiful castle with the beast."

"I'm not even pretty," Theresa whispered, "but I feel lonely already."

"And Mrs. Chinton is no beast," Miss Wilner said. "So there is no need to cry. I would stay longer if I did not have to make another visit in this house."

"Can't you stay until Mr. Chinton comes?" Mrs. Chinton asked as Miss Wilner said good-by to them in the hallway.

Miss Wilner said she would be back to visit in a few weeks. She put her arm around Theresa and reminded her of their agreement. "Remember that Beauty learned to love the beast, who was really very good and kind. Mr. and Mrs. Chinton are kind. They will be easy to love. Give them a chance."

Theresa sniffled her tears away. "You have to keep your promise, too," she said.

Miss Wilner grinned. "One look will tell you whether I've done that. I hope that the next time I see you, you'll only see a *part* of me."

"And you can ask Mrs. Chinton if I've been good . . ."

"We don't expect you to be good all the time," Mrs. Chinton said when she heard that. "All we want is what is good for you. We want to know that you are happy."

After Miss Wilner left—to see another client who lived nearby, she had said—Theresa had time to look at her foster mother. Mrs. Chinton was hardly taller than Theresa. Her hair had lots of gray in it and her face had many tiny lines around the eyes and the full lips. The veins on her hands showed that she had worked hard.

Theresa thought of her own mother's hands. They too had been veined and rough. But her own mother had not had a single gray hair, and her own mother had been tall and slender.

"Do I look very old to you, Theresa?"

Theresa shook her head. "Not very." Mrs. Gardiner had in some ways looked older than Mrs. Chinton did. Mrs. Chinton walked with her shoulders back and her head up. She looked almost as young as Val when she walked.

Together they unpacked all the boxes and hung up the skirts and blouses. Mrs. Chinton approved of the clothes. "That Miss Wilner is a fine person, for a white woman," she said. "But I like dealing with Mr. Dyson better. He understands our problems. It's always better to deal with one of our own kind."

Theresa dropped a hanger. "Does Miss Wilner know he's a Negro?" Mrs. Chinton nodded. Theresa wet her lips and asked, "Does anyone else know?"

"That he's a Negro?" She laughed at Theresa's shocked expression. "Of course. Didn't you know a black man could be a boss?"

Mrs. Chinton went on to tell Theresa about other Negroes who had become famous. Then she ended by saying, "My two sons, Donald and Fred, are going to have important jobs one day. Already they are teaching classes in a college. When you see them you will know why Dad and I are so proud of them."

Theresa kept changing her mind about her foster mother. At times Mrs. Chinton looked old and sounded old. Other times she looked and sounded like Val. When she talked about black people, she sounded a little like Val and a little like Tony. Her own mother had not liked to talk about color and in that way she was nothing like Mrs. Chinton. Yet, in another way her own mother sounded a lot like Mrs. Chinton. Both women wanted to keep to themselves.

"The only reason Dad got me to go to the agency was because I knew we could not get a child any other way. Mr. Dyson assured me that I was not letting myself in for any snooping social workers watching us. He said our privacy would be respected all the time."

Theresa noticed that the stiffness was going out of Mrs. Chinton's voice. She was talking faster and less crisply. Up to now she had sounded like a white person. Theresa was used to hearing grown-ups using their best speech when white people were around. It made being in this house feel more homelike when Mrs. Chinton stopped talking "white."

"What do you want me to do to help you now?" Theresa asked when her clothes were all put away.

"I hear you like to sew," Mrs. Chinton said. "How would you like to reinforce some of the buttons on your new coat and blouses? The way they sew things in the factories today is disgraceful."

She came into Theresa's room with a sewing box. "This weekend we'll have to get some fabric and pick a pattern. That is, if you'd like to make a dress . . ." She tried to read Theresa's face. "You know I've always dreamed of making dresses for a girl and perhaps I'm running ahead of myself."

"I'd love to make a dress for myself. Will you help me? I can make tiny tiny stitches. My mother taught me."

"Wonderful, Theresa," Mrs. Chinton said. "And I'll show you how to run a machine. I have a table model that I put on this desk."

"And you'll let me work it?" Theresa forgot that she had dreaded working on a sewing machine. She forgot her bad dream of heavy mops and dirty work.

"I'm looking forward to just that," Mrs. Chinton was saying when the outside door opened and a man called, "Marge, is she here?"

"In here, Philip. Theresa's in here," Mrs. Chinton called to him.

Theresa's mouth grew dry. She stepped behind Mrs. Chinton as a middle-sized man with a round face and lots of curly gray hair came toward her with his hand outstretched. His smile was so warm that Theresa slipped her hand right into his.

"A little girl, at last," he said. "Boys are grand and I'm not sorry I have two of them, but no home is a home without a girl. Isn't that so, Mother?"

"Especially a girl like Theresa," Mrs. Chinton exclaimed. "She is just like us. She likes to sew the way I do and she likes plants the way you do."

She led Mr. Chinton to Theresa's plant. Mr. Chinton looked from it to Theresa. "I'm glad you're not the kind of girl who treats plants as if they were not important. Some children forget that plants are living things. Now this one is sick and ailing, but it still has life in it. I'm happy to see that you love this plant enough to care for it even if it's not pretty."

Theresa felt proud of herself. No one had ever made her feel so special and grown-up. She looked up at Mr. Chinton without trying to hide her feelings. She liked Mr. Chinton and did not care who knew it.

Mr. Chinton changed his clothes and came into the living room. He found a book on the shelves and asked Theresa to look up the word "ivy" in the index. "We'll see what kind of soil ivy needs, and if I have it we can repot your plant before we have our dinner," he said.

She found the word. "Mr. Chinton," she said and stopped. He was making a face.

"Dad," he said. "Call me Dad."

"Dad," she repeated. It sounded good. She handed him the book and he read the planting directions aloud. He thought for a minute and then said he had everything they needed.

"Do you have to go down to the basement for the dirt?" Theresa asked.

"No, of course not," Mr. Chinton replied. "I have all my equipment out here on the terrace."

"Even the lawn mowers?" Theresa's eyes opened wide. This magic world she had been brought to was growing stranger by the minute. Imagine a janitor like Mr. Chinton who kept all of his tools on that tiny terrace.

Mr. Chinton stared at her. "What lawn mower?" he asked.

Mrs. Chinton came in from the kitchen. "Theresa, child, what did you ask Dad?"

Theresa repeated her question and Mrs. Chinton doubled up with laughter. "What do you think Dad does?" Between giggles she told Mr. Chinton that Theresa had thought she cleaned houses for white people. Theresa explained.

Mr. Chinton laughed as hard as his wife did. "All the gardening and janitorial work I do is in this apartment. I'm laughing because Mother made a similar mistake the first week we lived here."

He told her that Mrs. Chinton had seen a Negro woman cleaning windows on Sunday in an apartment across the court. Mrs. Chinton had called to him and exclaimed that "Some people are lucky enough to get help even on Sundays."

Mrs. Chinton grinned. "I guess all of us think that all Negroes can do is housework and such. That lady we saw was cleaning her own house."

Mr. Chinton explained that he worked in the post office. He had been transferred to the branch office that had been built in the cooperative. It was in the shopping center, which lay between the first and second group of buildings. The school Theresa was to attend was right behind the parking lot that surrounded the shopping center.

"This is the first time in my life that I do not have to ride to work in the subway. I feel like a king. I leave the house and walk right to my job," he said.

Theresa saw the way Mr. Chinton looked around at the room and at his wife. She saw Mrs. Chinton smile at him and then at her.

"That's the reason I let him talk me into moving here," she said. "When the children were small we dreamed of an apartment like this one—only not in a building full of white people. We were always crowded into three tiny rooms."

Mr. Chinton reminded her of some of the old apartments they had lived in before moving here. "Those were the days when mother worked in a slipcover factory. The days before I took the post office test. At that time I would no sooner get a job than I would lose it. Last hired—first fired."

"Tony Gardiner says it's always that way for black people," Theresa said. She understood all about losing jobs and living in small apartments. "I'll bet he doesn't know he could get a good job working in the post office if he studied hard and passed a test."

"Make sure to tell him," Mrs. Chinton told her. "Tell him to stay in school until he can pass some test."

"I will," Theresa promised. "And I'm going to tell him about this apartment."

"If he's like the boys coming into the post office from across the boulevard, you had better tell him to get used to working and living with white people. He'll need to know how to do that if he's going to work at any government job," Mr. Chinton said.

Mrs. Chinton frowned. She said something under her breath which sounded like, "It takes plenty of doing to make them get along with us."

"Marge, you've been unlucky in the white folks you've met," Mr. Chinton said. He stood up and pulled Theresa to her feet. "We had better get started on your plant before it gets dark outside. It will take too long to explain why Mother refuses to make friends with any white people. It has gotten so that she won't even make friends with any Negroes in this building if they're friends with the whites."

"I don't want my feelings hurt and I don't want to hurt anyone else's," Mrs. Chinton replied to Theresa's unspoken question. "I find it's best to mind my own business and let others mind theirs. Too many women around here are spending their time in meetings and clubs. I'd rather spend my time making some child happy. What do you say, darling?"

Theresa was watching her foster father's face. He started to say something but instead shut his lips tightly and called to Theresa to come out onto the terrace. He did not look kind now and Theresa shrank against her foster mother.

Out on the terrace, Mr. Chinton asked her to read the directions for transplanting ivy. Theresa turned to the proper page and tried to make out the small print. The words were long and unfamiliar. She stumbled over the first few words and then stopped reading.

Mrs. Chinton took the book from her. "Let me read it, darling. "You're probably tired and hungry. How can Dad expect you to read under such circumstances?"

Mr. Chinton frowned. "I'm trying to help her," he said to his wife. "I thought she would like the ivy transplanted today."

He whistled through his teeth tonelessly while he scooped soil onto a small table. He heaped some pebbles on a paper plate. "Let her pick a flowerpot," he said to Mrs. Chinton. "I hope you're not going to make her accept your ideas of what is nice in flowerpots, too."

Theresa realized that Mr. Chinton was annoyed at his wife because she had wanted Theresa to agree with her about keeping away from white people and people who went to meetings and clubs. She wondered why a grown man would be upset because a girl might agree with something his wife believed and he did not.

Theresa chose the orange pot quickly. She did not want him to think she was being influenced by Mrs. Chinton. He took the pot and set it on the table.

"Drop the pebbles in, Theresa," he said as he went into the house for her ivy.

He came back with the scraggly vines dragging on his arm. With a knife he swiftly loosened the dry soil from the pot. Bang! He hit the clump of soil off the roots.

Theresa could not take her eyes off the knife he held. Was he doing this because he was angry? She had carried her plant carefully all the way. Now he was banging it around as if he hated it and wanted to tear it apart.

Zip. Zip. The knife hacked a long root off the plant. Slash! Part of the vine came off.

"Stop that. That's enough," Theresa yelled. "That's my mother's plant. Give it to me."

She ripped the plant out of Mr. Chinton's hands and ran. She heard the pebbles and the orange pot come tumbling off the table as she raced through the living room and through the outside door out into the large hallway.

Where should she go? Where could she hide to get away from that knife? Where were the stairs? She could not wait for the elevator to come.

"Theresa, darling," Mrs. Chinton called.

"Theresa, child," Mr. Chinton called. "Come back here." He caught her arm and held her chin up so that he could see her face. "Did I frighten you? I saw how scared you looked when Mother talked about the white people."

"I wasn't scared of that." Theresa began to cry great round tears.

Mrs. Chinton stood with a watering can in her hands. "It was you who frightened her, Philip. She's not used to men and their gruff voices."

"Was it me?" Mr. Chinton asked. His face made Theresa's tears dry up. She had never seen a grownup look so sorry and so worried. "Child, I'm sorry. Mother

and I are used to arguing about what Negroes and white
. . . "

"Don't say Negroes," Mrs. Chinton said.

Mr. Chinton grinned. "All right. We argue about what Afro-Americans and white people ought to do about each other. Our sons are used to us, but you poor thing . . ." He hugged Theresa to him.

Theresa liked his shoulder and the smell of shaving cream. She let her head rest near his for a moment. "But you were angry enough to cut up my plant," she said mournfully.

Mrs. Chinton shook her head. "Dad was not really angry at me. He just doesn't answer me when he disagrees with me about people. And, sweety, he wasn't hurting your plant. He was cutting off the useless, dead stuff. When you transplant a plant you get rid of the sick stuff and leave only the healthy part. Tomorrow I'll read the whole instruction to you so that you will understand. Will you come in now?"

No one scolded about the broken pot or the spilled pebbles and soil. Mr. Chinton let Theresa pick another pot—a yellow one this time—and he watched her fill it properly. When he had cut all but a small root and stem away, he let Theresa press the sprig into the soil and water it.

"Will it grow big again?" Theresa asked as she replaced it on her shelf.

"Bigger and healthier than it ever was," Mr. Chinton said. "You give it plenty of good care and love it a lot and you'll see how well it will grow."

While Theresa washed up for dinner, she listened to

the quiet voices of her foster parents. How she missed the Gardiner household with the children talking in every room. Plants and pretty rooms were nice; her foster parents were nice, especially Mr. Chinton; but she felt cut off from everyone she knew and loved.

Mr. Chinton knocked on the bathroom door to tell her dinner was served. Theresa opened the door slowly. Mr. Chinton put his arm around her.

"I know how strange you must feel," he murmured. "You must feel as small and as hurt as your little ivy plant. But by tomorrow you'll have taken root here. We'll take care of you and we really want you very much."

Somehow, Theresa found it fairly easy to take her place at the table. Her foster parents seemed determined to make her forget her running away. They kept her talking about the Gardiner children and her mother. When dinner was over and the dishes done, Theresa admitted to herself that she had never enjoyed a dinner more than her first one in her new home.

Seven

While her foster parents watched a news program, Theresa wandered around the apartment from her room to the living room. It was sheer joy to feel the springy carpet. It was heavenly to run her hand over her smooth studio couch with its soft bedspread. She pirouetted in front of the mirror to see all the lovely colors in her room go around with her.

Her foster parents had turned off the news and were now talking in low voices. Mr. Chinton's deep voice made giggles spring up in her throat.

"He said he wants to be my dad . . ." she said to herself and repeated, "Dad."

Mrs. Chinton's clear, rather sharp voice reminded her a bit of a teacher's voice. "A nice teacher's," she quickly thought. She began to listen to the conversation.

They were talking about civil rights and black people. Nothing new. After church every Sunday she had heard much the same talk. People in church did not agree on what needed to be done and the Chintons, too, were not agreeing.

Mrs. Chinton, like her own mother, wanted people to mind their own business and live quietly and in peace. She did not want to mix with white people or even with what she called "Afro-Americans" who were tied up with white people.

Mr. Chinton said no man *"could* live alone even if he wanted to." He thought people ought to get together and work together. He was trying to convince her that his way was by far the better.

"If you gave yourself and this cooperative a real chance, if you let people make friends with you, you would see how fine people can be," he said.

Mrs. Chinton sniffed and replied, "Didn't I see how one of our fine white neighbors acted when she saw you in the laundry room? She walked in, took one look, saw a dark face, and ran."

Theresa became interested. This was the first time she had heard how white people acted toward black people in this building. What Mrs. Chinton was saying bore out the stories other people had told her.

Self-consciously she came into the living room and sat down on one of the soft chairs. The talk went on. Mr. Chinton was insistent in his belief that living to-

gether would bring trust and friendliness, and Mrs. Chinton kept saying that she was not going to expose herself to people's rudeness.

When they saw Theresa they stopped their argument. "Would you like to watch television?" Mr. Chinton asked her. "I don't know what programs children enjoy."

Mrs. Chinton looked in the paper. "I don't see anything worthwhile on. Perhaps you could read one of the boys' books."

Theresa did not dare say she would like to watch one of the programs some of the girls in school talked about. She did not dare say she hated to read. She lowered her eyes and said nothing.

Mr. Chinton chuckled. "What did you do at the Gardiners on the nights when you did not have to go to bed early? Since Mr. Dyson and Miss Wilner think you need to get used to us before you go to school, you can stay up tonight."

"I don't do anything special," Theresa answered. It was true. Her throat grew dry as she remembered the laughter and the teasing in the Gardiner home. The evenings had been filled with school talk and hair fixing.

And long before that—her eyes filled with tears—there had been the evenings with her mother. They would have been preparing the next night's dinner together and, by this time, the food would be on the stove and her mother would be telling her the factory gossip and laughing over the meanness of the forelady and the boss.

"Some nights," Theresa heard herself say, "Laura used to come up to my house and my mother used to help us cut out and sew dresses for Cookie's doll." How long ago that seemed. Had it ever happened at all?

Mr. Chinton asked about friends other than Laura, and Theresa confessed that she had none. "My mother didn't like me hanging around with a bunch of girls. She said too many kids together always meant mischief," Theresa said with a sigh.

Mrs. Chinton cleared her throat. "Your mother was a sensible woman. She brought you up well. But let's change the subject. You and I must get into Jamaica and get some fabric. We can begin making a dress for you tomorrow. How's that?"

She pulled Theresa to her feet and began to measure her so that they would get the right-sized pattern. When she had finished writing down the measurements, she touched Theresa's hair. "Why do you do this? It must take hours to put it up. Looks more like cardboard than hair when you're done," her foster mother said.

Up to her hair flew Theresa's fingers. She had considered her hair-do exceptionally nice. Val and Tony had both liked it. Did it look like cardboard?

Mr. Chinton's chuckle made her look at him. His smile made her brighten. "My daughter looks fine to me. She looks nicer than any girl I saw this week, or even this month." He winked at Theresa and came up to his wife and put his arm around her before he said, "Your new mother must like you very much indeed. She wants you to be just like her. And, since I happen to like your new mother very much, I can't say that she isn't looking out for both our welfares."

"I can wash my hair," Theresa said at once. "I can braid my hair if you like . . ." It was more to please Mr.

Chinton than to please her foster mother. His soft voice and his kind smiles made her warm inside.

Mrs. Chinton brought out towels and shampoo. "I think you can be showered and in your pajamas before nine o'clock when I expect your brothers to call. They always call after the rates change."

Theresa could not find her nightclothes. Six drawers she had to look through! In the thrill of so much space and so many pretty things, she almost forgot what she was looking for. When Mrs. Chinton called to tell her to hurry, she had to think twice to remember where she was going.

She put her light out with her pajamas in her arms and her soft flannel bathrobe tight around her thin body. Near the door was the shelf on which her plant stood in a place of prominence.

"Do you like it here as much as I do?" she whispered. "And are you as scared as I am that you'll do something wrong?" Her eyes adjusted to the darkness and she stared at the tiny sprig of ivy as if waiting for an answer. Her foster mother's call startled her out of her daydream and made her hurry toward the door.

While under the shower, Theresa made up a letter to Laura. *Have you ever lost your way to the bathroom?* she asked her friend. *I keep on forgetting where the doors are and where the chairs are. Maybe a fairy came and cast a spell and I'll wake up tomorrow and find it is all a dream.*

It did seem an impossible dream to be in a glass-enclosed shower with two washcloths and two towels laid out just for her own use. The quiet in the apartment after the noise of the Gardiner apartment added to the strangeness. Her own apartment on the fifth floor had never been this quiet because sounds from all over the building came into their apartment through the thin walls and floors.

Mr. Chinton knocked on the door and told her to hurry. "You'll miss talking to your brothers if you don't," he said.

She heard his voice and added another line to her imaginary letter. *And Laura, I like having a father. Dad, I'm going to call him. He's nice.*

Theresa came out of the bathroom with her hair wound up in a towel. She did not know where to go from there. Mrs. Chinton was in her room with a sewing box. The seams on Theresa's new slips were in need of a stitch or two to keep them from opening too soon.

"Mother wants to help you comb your hair," Mr. Chinton told her. He was behind the linen-closet door, shining her new shoes.

Theresa put her hand out, "I'll do that." She wondered if she had already scuffed the toes or dirtied the leather. "I didn't know they were dirty."

"They're not," Mr. Chinton answered. "I like to put a good coat of polish on new shoes to protect them. You can keep shoes looking new much longer if you keep them highly shined."

"Thank you," Theresa said politely. She wished Miss Wilner had told her what you were to say to foster parents when they did extra special things for you. "Thank you," was not half enough to say.

Mrs. Chinton combed her hair into four sections. She

twisted the sections this way and that until she was satisfied. "How do you like this?" she said at last. Theresa looked into the mirror. Mrs. Chinton had pulled one front section back and had joined it to the two back sections. Theresa nodded. A pony tail was not too bad. However, the other front section was to be braided so as to fall down the side of her head.

Like a baby's, Theresa thought.

"Like a plume," Mr. Chinton said. He made an arc with his hand and explained. "Great ladies used to wear feathered plumes on their hats that used to drape their faces and make them look mysterious and interesting."

Theresa looked again. The braid was lying along her cheek, thick and wiry. Did it make her look interesting? Her face went up so that she could see herself better.

Mrs. Chinton stood back approvingly. "Now you look proud of yourself. A black girl has nothing to be ashamed of. She doesn't have to copy anyone. What she is and what she looks like is what God in his wisdom made her to be."

"My mother always said something like that, too," Theresa said, "but she didn't like nappy hair . . ." She was trying to be satisfied with her hair. Mr. and Mrs. Chinton liked it this way and she ought to please them.

"What's the matter, Theresa?" Mr. Chinton asked as he came in with a briefcase in his hands. It was clear that the briefcase had never been used and that he was giving it to her. How could Theresa tell him she preferred smooth hair to braids?

"Nothing is the matter," Theresa answered. "I'm thinking of how good you are to me."

Her foster parents brushed her thanks aside. They acted as if she were giving them more than they gave her. Mr. Chinton winked and asked Theresa if she thought old folks dull. "So you see we two old folks now have something to wake us out of our dullness. And that something is you," he said and chucked her under the chin.

The briefcase was something they were eager to get out of their closet, Mrs. Chinton said. Donald had gotten it as a graduation present when he got out of high school. It had been lying unused for four years.

"You see how useful you are?" Mr. Chinton asked. "That is, if girls nowadays use these things."

Theresa found a small stapler, a ruler, a compass, and a fully equipped pencil case in the briefcase. Mr. Chinton grinned with embarrassment when Theresa asked if Donald had gotten all of this in the briefcase. "I didn't think boys in college used crayons and such," she said with wonder. Val had given her a picture of college that sounded like all work with no time for drawing and coloring.

Mrs. Chinton looked fondly at her husband. "Dad must have bought that for you," she said to Theresa. "It is a little present."

The telephone rang and Theresa felt herself propelled out of her room and into the kitchen. She held her breath while both her foster parents talked to both Fred and Donald.

"Your turn," Mr. Chinton said. "Say hello to your brother, Fred. He's the older one."

Fred said he was in Chicago. He asked her how she liked the place his father had chosen to live in. "Write and tell me about yourself and all about the friends you make," he said. He offered to teach her to ride a bike if she promised to show him around the cooperative when he came home for the Christmas holidays.

"I've always wanted a sister," he said before he gave the phone over to Donald.

Mrs. Chinton told her to ask Donald if he minded giving up the briefcase. Donald heard his mother and laughed. "For a sister I would not mind giving up dinner for a week," he said, with a full laugh that reminded Theresa of Mr. Chinton's. He promised to write to Theresa that week and ended with another laugh. "Watch Mother for us," he said. "And watch to see that she doesn't keep you studying all the time. Make friends that have older sisters so that Fred and I will have lots of dates on our holiday. Is it a deal?"

Theresa almost fainted with pleasure. Brothers. Fred and Donald had called her "sister." They wanted her in the family.

"Dad," she said to Mr. Chinton as he hung up the phone for her. "Donald said I should give you a kiss for him."

Mr. Chinton leaned down and presented her with his cheek. Putting a kiss there was one of the easiest things Theresa had ever done.

"You, too," she said to Mrs. Chinton. "Donald said I was to give you one for him." She could not say "Mother" and the kiss she gave had none of the warmth she meant to put into it. The feel of her mother's cheek came vividly to mind and spoiled the kiss.

It was another Theresa who went to bed that night in

the blue-and-white room on a wide studio couch. She memorized where her slippers were under the bed and where the light switch was on the wall. In the dark she tried to recall the number of steps it took to get to the door and the direction of the bathroom.

Tomorrow Mrs. Chinton was going to show her around the neighborhood and take her into Jamaica to buy material and a pattern for a dress.

But Theresa could not fall asleep. She tossed in the bed and wished Laura and Cookie were near her. Mrs. Chinton had said that she might read in bed if she wanted to. Theresa found the light and a book with lots of pictures. It was about a boy named Hans and a pair of skates. Theresa could not follow the story because too many of the words were too hard. After a while, she put out the light and shut her eyes with determination.

Sleep did not come. She kept thinking about her day. So many odd happenings. *Would Laura believe me,* she wondered. Tony would think she was making up stories. He did not know that black people could be bosses of whites and that they could live in houses with white people and have rugs all over the floors and terraces with plants and flowers.

Like the movies. Theresa sighed. She pinched her leg hard. The leg was real and the pinch hurt. But nothing else felt real.

Theresa had an idea. She quickly put on the light and ran to the mirror on the closet door.

"Maybe I've turned white now," she said to herself with a giggle. "I better look."

"Theresa?"

Mrs. Chinton tried the door and came in when Theresa answered. "Can't you sleep, child?" she asked.

Mrs. Chinton wore a robe. She looked softer and younger. She drew Theresa back into bed and tucked the covers around her.

"You must miss your friends," Mrs. Chinton said. "Poor child. Someday soon I hope I can meet all the Gardiners. They were very nice to you in your need."

Theresa found herself tightening up. Mrs. Chinton was talking softly. Pity was in her voice and Theresa could not stop her back from tingling with annoyance.

"Lie back, child," Mrs. Chinton said. "This has been a long day. You're not used to being alone."

The light went out and Mrs. Chinton's voice went on in the dark. The pity was still there but the words were like a sad song.

"My mother died when I was fifteen. I know how empty you feel. I cried and cried. My aunt kept me and I loved her and she loved me. She made me talk to her about my mother. She didn't want me to forget . . ."

"I cried, too," Theresa heard herself say. Her eyes filled with tears. "Crying doesn't help. I'm still an orphan."

"Tell me about your hurt. My aunt taught me to share my pain and my happiness. Sharing lessens the one and doubles the other. We Afro-Americans had to find that truth out for ourselves many times."

"Am I an Afro-American?" Theresa asked. In school she had learned that Africa was a large continent. She had seen pictures of the jungles and of people in short skirts. "I don't want to be one of those."

Mrs. Chinton took her hand. "The white people do not tell us that Africans have a long and wonderful history, too. But we know that our people brought to this world a great many things. Tomorrow you and I will find a book and read of the things black men did before the white man came and enslaved him. And now in Africa we see pride and a desire to find freedom for all men."

She talked softly. Theresa believed her and her heart seemed to grow larger and stronger. Once in church she had heard a man talk about Africa. She had thought that talk just church stuff and meant to make you good.

"In this apartment, after today," Theresa whispered, "I—I can almost believe that"— her voice got stuck and she had to wait until it cleared itself before she finished softly—"that it's not too bad being b-bl-black."

Mrs. Chinton kissed her cheek. "We have lots to be proud of. We have lots to hope for and pray for."

"Oh, I wish my mommy could be here now," Theresa cried. "She'd like you. Really she would."

"I'm sure I would have liked her. Now little one, to sleep. Shall I sing to you?"

"She was so pretty," Theresa moaned. "She wanted me to go to school and get smart. Only . . . only I didn't listen to her. I didn't do my homework lots of times and I was so dumb . . . too . . ."

"Sh, Theresa. You did the best you could. We all do what we can. Quiet, child, or you'll wake Dad." She stroked Theresa's forehead and began to sing a soft lullaby about sheep and the Lord.

Theresa shut her eyes. Everything in the room grew distant as the song grew softer and softer. "Is my mother watching?" Theresa murmured into the darkness.

The song went on. The lost sheep were on their way home. "Miss Wilner says this is only a temporary home," Theresa whispered.

Into the song came an answer, "We do what we can, child. For your sake I'll try."

"Sing more about the sheep, Mother." Theresa curled under the blanket. "Make them come home, please make them all—come—home . . ."

Theresa was sound asleep.

Eight

The next three days flew by all too quickly. On Friday she went to Jamaica with her foster mother. They bought a blue fabric that looked like silk and a woolen plaid fabric for a jumper. The blue would make both a blouse to go with the jumper and a dress for church. They spent a long time in the library afterwards finding books and stories about Africa.

"Now wasn't that fun?" Mrs. Chinton asked, and Theresa had to admit that even the visit to the library had been nice.

While Mrs. Chinton started dinner, Theresa insisted on dusting all the furniture. "And I can clean a bathroom very well, too," Theresa said with her head high.

She worked the way her mother had taught her to. After dusting she washed the cloth and hung it up to dry. In the bathroom she washed and then polished all the chromium and the porcelain until it shone.

When Mr. Chinton came home, Mrs. Chinton led him through the house, "See how clean our house is. Isn't our girl a wonder!"

Mr. Chinton praised Theresa until she blushed. He promised to let her water even his most precious violets. "You're an exceptionally dependable girl," he said.

After dinner Theresa listened to the news with her foster parents. "I want to do what you do," she said, when Mr. Chinton told her she did not have to join the family in their nightly after-dinner routine.

When the program was over, she got one of her library books. Carefully she sounded out the words and tried to follow the story, but her eyes began to close and the story kept escaping her.

"Let me read for you," Mr. Chinton took the book and led her to the ottoman. Resting on his knees, she listened to the story of a small African boy who had come to study in a big school in an African city.

"I didn't know there were cities in Africa," Theresa said, when the story was over. She wanted to hear more about Africa and the children there.

Mrs. Chinton promised to read another story with her before bedtime. *This is better than the movies,* Theresa thought as she pored over the pictures in her new book. She hated to stop looking and put the book down even when Mrs. Chinton brought out the pretty material and the patterns for her new clothes.

Sewing with Mrs. Chinton did not turn out to be as much fun as it had been with her mother. Her mother had always chattered about the people in her factory. Theresa had learned to know each woman who worked there by name. She knew all the family stories that her mother had been told. This was the time she told her mother all that had happened that day in school. With Mrs. Chinton the talk was all about politics and the leaders of the black people.

Mr. Chinton called his wife a "black nationalist." Mrs. Chinton bristled. "I'm nothing of the kind. I'm no joiner and I never will be one," she told Theresa firmly.

"I was only teasing," Mr. Chinton admitted. "Now let's talk about something of more interest to Theresa. Let's talk about our children."

Mrs. Chinton was willing. She began to tell stories about Fred and Donald. Each story she began was finished by Mr. Chinton. Theresa had to laugh at the way they told the stories. Mrs. Chinton would go up to a certain part and then she would turn to her husband and say, "You finish it, Philip . . . I simply have no words left."

From the stories and the album of old pictures they brought out, Theresa learned about her foster brothers. She felt comfortable enough to tell the Chintons that Val Gardiner wanted to meet the boys.

"She'll like them," Theresa said warmly. "The boys are real nice."

"And if you like Valerie, then I'm sure she's nice, too," Mr. Chinton said as he put away his pictures.

As promised, Mrs. Chinton read another story from

the library book before they sent Theresa to bed that night. They wanted Theresa to be up early the next day. Saturday was marketing day and they liked to shop before the stores got too crowded.

Saturday, Theresa went with her foster parents to the supermarket in the cooperative. Then she helped unpack the bundles and make the salad for their lunch. After lunch they did the dishes. Then they all went for a walk around the cooperative.

The circle in which their building stood began to look familiar. She remembered where Miss Wilner had parked her car and where the path to the shopping center was. She walked between her foster parents with light, springy steps.

They pointed out the post office where Mr. Chinton worked and the school where Theresa would be going on Monday. They named the streets that divided the cooperative from the rest of the neighborhood.

In her new coat and hat Theresa was warm and proud as she looked around and saw the many children—most of them white—who were playing in the playgrounds. No one seemed to pay her any attention and she felt free to look as long as she wished to.

She went through five circles. Each one had a flower garden in the center and two playgrounds within its boundaries. There were three schools and a community center on the property. She saw them all.

Mrs. Chinton did not think much of the community center. Too much mixing of white and black went on there for her taste. Mr. Chinton did not think much of the center, either. But for the opposite reason.

"Children from outside the cooperative are not allowed to join any of the clubs," he said. "That discourages Negro children from across the boulevards from playing with our children. I don't like that," he said as he led the way back to their own building.

Theresa eyed the few black children she passed. *Would she ever meet anyone to be friends with?* One of the girls standing near her building looked at her hard as she came into the building with the Chintons. The girl looked as if she lived there and was wondering about Theresa.

"That girl lives here," Mr. Chinton remarked. "I've met her father. He's a lawyer and comes into the post office often."

"She looks about your age," Mrs. Chinton said. "Perhaps you can meet her and go to school with her."

Theresa thought the girl looked rather uninteresting. She wore glasses and seemed nosy. Theresa had glanced back and caught the girl's eyes going from her own small figure to her foster parents broader ones.

She was glad to be back in the apartment. The rest of the day went by speedily with more stories and sewing. She had her blouse cut and basted before she went to bed that night.

Sunday was much like the Sundays she had always known. The church the Chintons attended was not in a store, but the service and the sermon were familiar. Theresa spent her time looking at the ladies and the girls.

After services, Mr. Chinton introduced Theresa to some girls her own age. Politely she listened to their talk about people and things she knew nothing of, until the Chintons were ready to go home. On the way, she sat alone in a seat on the bus and watched the streets go by.

No work was done in the Chinton home on Sundays. The day was warm and sunny. She sat out on the terrace with her foster parents after dinner.

"Bored, Theresa?" Mr. Chinton asked as he exchanged sections of the paper with his wife.

"No," Theresa answered. She wasn't. Not a bit of it. She was busy making up another letter to Laura in her mind. She wanted to tell Laura that she could go on sitting in the sun forever. She did not want to awaken from her dream.

Darkness and chill made the family go into the house and shut the door. Theresa went into her room. Tomorrow was school. The dream might be over then. At home she could do everything the Chintons expected of her. In school—NEVER.

She touched the sprig of ivy. *I wish I never had to go to school.* She fingered the crisp leaf. It felt strong and alive as if it were trying to answer her. "I know," Theresa murmured aloud. "You're telling me that I'm always expecting the worst. Wasn't I scared that you were going to be dead? And aren't you alive and getting stronger?"

She grinned at herself. She recalled that even coming here had frightened her. *Maybe school won't be as bad as I expect, either,* she said firmly to herself as she prepared to shower and lay out her things as her foster mother had asked her to do.

"As long as you live and get stronger and more beautiful each day," she told her ivy as she passed it, "I'm going to believe only in good things happening."

First thing next morning, Theresa jumped out of bed to look at her plant. It had not grown much, but it was shiny and straight; definitely alive.

"Then I'm going to believe that I'm going to like *this* school," she said. A peek in the mirror on the door told her she looked bright and alive, too.

She dressed in the skirt and blouse she had not worn yet. Except for her hair, she thought she looked well. When she brushed her hair and redid her braid she made sure it was pushed far back on her head where it might escape notice.

Breakfast was hurried. Mrs. Chinton set the dishes in a soaking pan and put on her coat.

"Maybe I had better walk you two ladies to the school," Mr. Chinton said when Theresa went for her coat. "You both look grand and someone may decide to kidnap you."

Mrs. Chinton laughed, but Theresa was too nervous to do anything but smile a sickly smile. The weekend had ended too soon—she wished schools had never been invented.

Down in the lobby she almost lost courage completely. Near the letter boxes a group of white boys and girls were gathered around a notice that was tacked on a bulletin board.

Mr. Chinton took her arm and pulled her down the hall gently. "The Negro Civic Club is planning to give the operetta *The Mikado*," he said. "They want actors, actresses, musicians, stage hands, singers, dancers, and people who can sew."

"Why are *they* interested if it's the Negro Civic Club?" Mrs. Chinton asked when they were near the outside doors. Theresa wondered, too. From behind her she heard the young voices raised in laughter.

One boy said in a loud voice, "What makes them think that any white kid will want to be in one of their plays?"

Theresa and Mrs. Chinton straightened as if a cord had been attached to their spines. Mr. Chinton chuckled. "Same kind of thinking *you* do, Marjorie," he said to his wife. "That's the kind of thinking the Negro Civic Club wants to get rid of."

"When it succeeds in getting rid of it on *that* side, it will be time enough for them to worry about getting rid of it on *our* side," Mrs. Chinton said curtly.

The paths were full of children going to school. When she had seen the white children in the playgrounds, Theresa had thought them rather ordinary. Dressed for school and going in her direction, they looked terrifying.

"I know how you feel." Mrs. Chinton pressed her hand. "Don't worry about them. Mind your own business and they won't bother you. If anyone ever annoys you, go right to the post office and find Dad at the stamp window."

Theresa felt better. She said good-by to Mr. Chinton at the mall and went on with her foster mother with firmer steps. The post office was halfway between the school yard and her house. She would not have too far to run for help, should she need it.

A truck was pulling away from the area near the school yard. It had finished depositing a two-story high pile of topsoil in the large area between the mall and the parking lot.

From all directions children were running toward the topsoil hill. White boys and Negro boys came tearing up one side of the hill and tumbling, rolling down the other. One white boy in particular seemed to be doing more pushing than the others, but Theresa had no time to see whom he was pushing.

Mrs. Chinton glared at all the boys. "Mothers ought to supervise their children more closely," she said. "Look at those boys getting filthy before school."

Several boys came bouncing down almost at her feet. Theresa jumped back to avoid them. She agreed when Mrs. Chinton said, "Dangerous. Those boys might have broken their legs or yours."

Theresa kept to the far side of the path. Too many white boys and girls were heading toward the school gate. Remembering the talk of the white children in her building, Theresa cringed each time someone's shoulder brushed hers. She came through the gate with her foster mother just as the line-up buzzer sounded.

From every side boys came running. She and Mrs. Chinton had no time to step aside as two boys pounded into the yard almost side by side. One of them was white, the other black. Both were covered with topsoil. In their hurry the boys almost knocked Mrs. Chinton off her feet.

The white boy did not look back when he passed Mrs. Chinton and in his hurry to get to the line he shoved into the other boy hard enough to unbalance him.

Before the black boy could get straightened out, a teacher's voice blasted through a loudspeaker, "Jonathan Thompson. Apologize to that lady. How dare you run in the school yard."

The boy sullenly turned to Mrs. Chinton. "Sorry," he murmured. He then strode to his line. Theresa looked after him in time to see the other boy—the white boy—looking at Jonathan and grinning.

Theresa followed her foster mother toward the school entrance. She had trouble making her legs move. Had she dared, Theresa would have spun around and run miles from this school. All schools were awful, but this one with its billions of white children was truly dangerous. Not even Miss Wilner would expect her to walk right into such a place.

Not a hint of Theresa's true feelings showed. Mrs. Chinton had her hand on Theresa's elbow and Theresa went with her into the school. Breathing was painful, but Theresa kept her courage up. *I promised Miss Wilner I was not going to run before I was sure . . . I promised and I'm going to do it,* she said over and over to herself as she walked into the general office.

Nine

After Theresa's transfer had been attended to, the secretary sent them into the principal's office. Mrs. Chinton went in first.

Theresa heard the principal greet her foster mother warmly. He told her that this school was integrated and that the feeling within it was fairly good.

Mrs. Chinton made a small sound in her throat. "All I expect a school to do is to get my child ready for college. I'm not interested in integration or in politics." She told the principal that she had two sons who were doing post-graduate work.

The principal talked about the necessity for children

to live together and respect each other. Again Mrs. Chinton made a small sound of disagreement. "Impossible," she said. She told the principal about the club advertisement. "My poor child almost fell through the floor when she heard those children read the poster and laugh at it."

The principal said that he was doing all he could to promote that operetta in the school. Mrs. Chinton thought it a waste of time. "What I do think you might do is to keep the boys off that pile of topsoil dumped in the parking lot near the school," she said. "We can't do anything about changing the world, but we can do something about keeping the children from breaking their necks."

"I'll look into it at once," the principal said in a voice that promised action.

It was Theresa's turn next. The principal tested her reading and said her word-attack skills were fairly good. "What she needs is the experiences that build vocabulary and an opportunity for wide reading," he told Mrs. Chinton. He assigned Theresa to a better class than she rated. "Since your mother will work with you, I'll give you a chance in class 6-543. It will mean a lot of work, but I think you'll manage."

Mrs. Chinton followed the monitor up the stairs. Theresa kept close to her. She was proud of the way her foster mother had talked to the principal. She was glad that her foster mother had reported what the white kids in the building had said about the Negro Junior Civic Club, whatever that was.

Part of her class number, 543, was her room number. Theresa looked into the room expectantly. A roomful of white faces. Her head went down, but not before she had seen one dark face. The face of the boy who had bumped into them in the yard—Jonathan Thompson.

The teacher was pointing her finger at him and asking him how long she was going to have to keep him near her desk. "When are you going to stop your running and your fighting?" the teacher asked. She stopped talking as Mrs. Chinton came into the room.

"Finish the arithmetic problems on the board and then take out a book and read until I'm ready for you," she ordered the class.

Softly she greeted Theresa. "I'm Mrs. Jennet," she said after the monitor left.

Turning to Mrs. Chinton she said, "I'm embarrassed every time I see one of our boys making a spectacle of himself."

Our boys! Theresa looked at the teacher. How had she missed seeing that Mrs. Jennet was a Negro? Was it because she was yelling at a black boy in front of all these white kids? And because she had not caught the white boy?

While Mrs. Jennet wrote out the list of assignments Theresa had missed, Theresa took a quick look at the room. The double desks were arranged in three groups. In each group eight children sat facing each other, four facing the windows, four facing the closets. Six children sat in single seats. Jonathan was the only one facing the board. His chair was right next to the teacher's desk. Theresa knew why he was there.

Mrs. Chinton left and Mrs. Jennet introduced Theresa

to the class. She asked a white girl to change her seat so that "tiny Theresa" could sit close to the board. Front seat near the door was to be Theresa's.

Theresa did not lift her head to see who her seat partner was. All she could see of the girl were two white hands. She marveled at them as they cleared space on the desk for her books.

Were all white hands so uniform in color back and palm? Her own hands were much darker on the nail side than they were on the palm side. She hid her hands quickly.

She turned to put her coat away in the closet and had her first good look at the class. She spotted the dark faces immediately. They were spread around the room among the white ones. In back was the tall girl with glasses; she was flat-faced and looked like a frog. There was a husky boy with longish hair, and a skinny boy with close-cropped hair. Near the windows a pretty girl with bangs sat nibbling on a pencil. Four, so far, not counting Jonathan and herself.

In the middle of the room Theresa saw the white boy who had come running into the yard with Jonathan, the boy who had pushed him aside as he ran to the class line. Theresa looked away from him fast. He had caught her glance and began to smirk. She almost missed seeing the girl who sat at a single desk in the center of the room.

The girl was huddled low in her seat. Her hair was matted and greasy-looking; her neck needed washing and her dress was missing a button. It was held together with a safety pin.

Theresa always wondered about girls who did not keep

themselves clean. She felt like taking this girl into the bathroom and scrubbing her. She dropped her eyes to avoid meeting those of the girl she was examining. Only the girl was not looking in Theresa's direction. She was looking sideways toward the white boy who had been with Jonathan.

The boy was holding up a picture he had drawn on a page from his loose-leaf notebook. He had his face turned front so that he could see Mrs. Jennet.

One by one children lifted their heads, looked at the picture, suppressed a giggle, and then looked down at their work again.

Theresa stared at the artwork: a picture of an ape scratching his underarms. "Another one?" the caption under the picture read.

The frog-faced girl met Theresa's eyes. With her lips the girl said, "Ignore him. He's a nut."

Theresa walked to her seat with shaky knees. She would be glad to ignore the boy, but the class had not. They were all laughing at her behind their books. Mrs. Chinton had cause to keep away from white people. No one liked being called an ape.

Concentrating on arithmetic and spelling was hard when she kept thinking she heard someone tittering about her looks.

The class was given a ten-minute recess in the middle of the morning. Her neighbor, Julie Fisher, was told by Mrs. Jennet to introduce Theresa to the girls.

The white girl put out her hand. "I know how you feel. I've changed schools in the middle of a term and it's awful."

Blue eyes met Theresa's black ones. They were friendly, but Theresa kept her hand at her side. While she followed the white girl to the other side of the room she studied the girl's face. It was a lovely face with a sprinkling of freckles. It was hard not to feel the warmth that radiated from this girl. It was hard not to want to touch the thick, honey-colored braids that danced over her shoulders as she walked.

They came to the desk where the pretty, colored girl sat. This was Sharon. The frog-faced girl, Dena, was sitting on the other girl's desk. They were talking about Jonathan and the unfair way Mrs. Jennet had scolded him without finding out who the other boy had been.

"Maybe she didn't see Bert," Dena said as Julie and Theresa came over.

"She never sees anything that Bert does," the pretty girl said sullenly. She stopped talking so that Julie could introduce Theresa.

Theresa memorized the names. Sharon was the pretty one. Frog-face was Dena Toler.

Dena stared at Theresa. "Didn't I see you going into our building one day? Do you live there?"

Julie said, "How nice. I live in that building, too." They each told the section they lived in. Julie lived in the middle section one floor beneath the Chintons. Dena lived in the front section.

Sharon seemed displeased that Theresa lived in the development. She said something over her shoulder to the girl with the safety pin stuck in her dress. Theresa heard her call that girl, "Hattie."

Dena leaned over toward Hattie and said in a loud

whisper, "Hattie, why don't you get a needle and thread and sew a button on your dress?"

Julie in an equally loud whisper said, "Why don't you mind your own business?"

Sharon and Hattie laughed, and to Theresa's surprise Dena laughed, too. The tall girl shook her head. "My mother says that Julie is the protector of the weak."

"I am not," Julie said. "I just happen to like Hattie."

Hattie smiled at the white girl and the white girl started what appeared to be a smile. She quickly covered her mouth before the smile spread too wide. But not before Theresa saw what the hand was hiding.

Instead of teeth all that could be seen was a mouthful of wires.

Dena saw Theresa's expression and laughed. "Julie is wearing braces. The dentist put them on to keep her teeth straight."

Pity for the girl who had to wear such ugly things in her mouth made Theresa come closer to the white girl. She was glad when Julie said it was time to meet the rest of the gang.

Carefully Theresa noted the names of the girls she met. The white girl with the brown wavy hair was Jennie. She walked home with Julie. Paul was a white boy who lived in the third building in their circle. He was talking about the operetta that the civic club was going to give. He asked Julie if she were going to be in it.

Theresa listened to hear whether any these of boys or girls would laugh about the operetta or the club. No one seemed to be at all interested in what Paul was saying. No one laughed.

Then Julie introduced her to Jonathan; to Bob, a husky boy; and to a skinny boy, Kenneth. The boys were whispering about Bert when she came over.

Jonathan asked her where she had gone to school before. When she said "Harlem," he envied her. "I'd a million times rather go to school down there. No Berts, there."

Bob and Kenneth said they ought to get together and "take care of" Bert and his friends. Julie shook her head. "Jonny has to keep out of fights until this operetta is over. His father will be sore as blazes if he gets into trouble again."

"Aw, all you want is for Jonny to get the part of the guitar-playing prince in that show," Bob said to Julie.

Kenneth pretended to strum a guitar and sing. Julie laughed behind her hand. "I guess you're right, Bob," she said. "My parents and Jonny's say that he'll be a great actor if he works at it."

Kenneth frowned. "Who'll come and see that old play? I heard some kids down in the school yard making fun of the club and the play."

Jonathan balled up his fists. "That's Bert's doing. He's telling all the Dukes to tear down our club posters and keep away from the club. He doesn't want any of the white kids joining us."

"Then what good is the play?" Julie asked. "My father said this play will bring all the kids together."

Kenneth and Bob said that there was no play in the world that could bring whites and blacks together.

"And what we had better do right quick is to get our fists on Bert and his gang. Those Dukes are up to no good and we have to stop them," Bob said heatedly.

"Sh. Sh. Sh." Julie whispered, "Mrs. Jennet will hear you."

"I don't care if she does hear me," Bob answered. "It's time she caught on to Bert. She and this school and that cooperative all give me a swift pain . . ."

It was time to get back to work. Julie led Theresa back to their places. Under her breath, she explained Bob's anger. "The management of the cooperative does not allow outsiders—that means the Negro kids in the neighborhood, like Bob and Sharon and Kenneth and Hattie, to join any of the clubs or activities that take place in the community center."

Theresa's head ached by the time she came back to her seat. Social studies was peaceful after all the talk she had heard. She turned the pages of her textbook as if she were reading and thought over what had been said.

As Mrs. Jennet called on children for answers, Theresa tried to fit voices to names. Dena was the tall one— frog-face. Dena seemed to know lots of answers. Mrs. Jennet complimented her twice. Paul had a deep voice. He was the white boy who wanted to be in the operetta. Jennie and Hattie both missed an answer and Sharon was the one at the board making a list of the continents.

No one seemed to be paying any attention to her and she sat back in her seat and let her mind wander to Harlem and the Gardiners. Almost lunchtime. Laura would be waiting for Cookie soon.

"Lunch bell, Theresa." Julie prodded Theresa on the shoulder.

Theresa sat up. Had Mrs. Jennet noticed her daydreaming? Mrs. Jennet did not say anything until the class was in line. Then she asked if anyone was going to Theresa's building. Julie and Dena both raised their hands and Mrs. Jennet asked them to take care of their new classmate.

"We'll try," Julie said brightly, when, from the back of the line someone called, "Why? Think the zookeepers will get her?"

Mrs. Jennet was furious. Her face grew stern. "Who said that?" she snapped.

"Kenny did," Bert called out.

There was a gasp from the class. Theresa bit into her lip to keep it steady. Everyone knew that Bert had called out those words. Everyone but the teacher knew that.

Mrs. Jennet made Kenneth get out of the line. Jonathan sprang to Kenneth's side. "He did not say that. Why should Kenny say such a thing?"

Mrs. Jennet shrugged her shoulders. "I can't imagine. You boys have such strange ideas of humor I don't put anything past you."

She made Jonathan get back in line and then she led the class down the stairs. She kept Kenneth after the class was out of the building.

Jonathan grabbed Bert by the coat collar as soon as they were out of the school gate. "You better tell Mrs. Jennet or I'll push your teeth in."

"I thought Kenny said that . . . I didn't know he didn't say it," Bert said with such an innocent face that Theresa almost believed him.

"Rat," Jonathan said and threw Bert over toward the sand that bordered the parking lot.

Dena, Julie, and several white children began pulling Jonathan onto the path. They said Bert had no sense and no decency.

"Leave him alone. Don't dirty your hands on him," the white boy, Paul, said as he pushed Jonathan as far from Bert as he could.

Jonathan began to walk home with his group. Everyone was talking at once. Theresa remained on the side at the end of the group walking in her direction. They were saying that any change in the class set Bert off. Suddenly Julie turned around. "Where's Theresa. We forgot Theresa."

Jonathan spun around. "Did Bert get to her?" Bert was running wildly up the side of the topsoil hill. Jonathan made a full circle and saw Theresa near the fence.

"Here she is, Julie. Come on Th-re-sa," he called.

Julie corrected him. "Ta-re-sa. The 'h' doesn't sound. Isn't that right?"

Theresa nodded. She was sorry they had missed her. She didn't like everyone looking at her.

Jonathan remained at her side. He practiced her name several times and then shook his head. "What a serious name for such a tiny girl. Haven't you got another name? A pet name?"

With every eye on her, Theresa could not get her tongue to move. She felt her legs getting ready to run away. She even started forward when she remembered her promise to Miss Wilner. She stood still.

"T-T-Tweedy," she stammered. She hoped he would not laugh or say it was a baby name.

He didn't laugh. He listened, said it, and chuckled.

"Nice name. Dainty-like. Makes me think of a bird." He called to the others, "Hey kids, doesn't she remind you of a tiny bird?"

Theresa thanked Miss Wilner silently. She was glad she had controlled herself. The group was walking ahead again, talking about Kenny and Bert. She let herself walk alongside Jonathan and Julie. When she got upstairs she would look up "dainty" in the dictionary. She hoped it meant something like pretty.

Ten

Delicious and choice, the dictionary said about dainty. Theresa came to the table wondering how those adjectives applied to her. She ate her sandwich thoughtfully.

"Have a good morning?"

"I guess," Theresa answered. Since no schoolday was particularly good, she had to consider this a good one. The teacher had not called on her and she had not made a single wrong answer.

"Who walked home with you?"

"A lot of kids that live in this section," Theresa answered truthfully. She did not mention that part of the way she had walked all alone.

Mrs. Chinton asked whether there had been any announcement about the topsoil hill and Theresa had to say that there had been none.

"The principal promised to tell the children to keep off, but I suppose he's forgotten by now," Mrs. Chinton said with disappointment.

She was disappointed, too, that no announcement had been made about the operetta or the Negro Junior Civic Club. "Not that I take any stock in that sort of nonsense," she said. "But I did not like to hear some of those fresh children making fun of the club." She did not ask about Theresa's classmates and Theresa offered no information.

After lunch, her elevator came down to the ground floor almost at the same moment that the even one did. Julie and Jonathan greeted her and all three walked down the long hall to where Dena was already waiting.

Dena began talking as soon as she saw them. "I told my mother about Bert and she said that if Mrs. Jennet punishes Kenny it will be a disgrace. She says we have to tell her about Bert."

"I'm not a tattletale," Julie said with fire in her eyes.

Jonathan said that if Kenneth were punished he would beat Bert up. Theresa walked by herself, close enough to hear what was said, yet out of the way.

When Paul and Jennie joined the group, they agreed with Dena. The group finally decided that if Mrs. Jennet let Kenneth go without any punishment, they would forget the episode. However, if Kenneth had to go to the principal's office, or had to do extra homework, then Dena would go up to Mrs. Jennet and tell her the truth.

The talk then shifted to plans for getting more white children to try out for the operetta. Julie thought that each club member ought to try to get one new member by being extra nice to someone.

Jonathan suggested that Dena, who was tops in the class in math, should volunteer to help everyone who joined the club.

Paul put his hand up. "I'm the first one to join then. When can I get my first lesson?" Everyone laughed at Paul's sigh when Dena said she could not teach without a license.

Theresa kept glancing about to see if the children coming along noticed the white girls in her group. Julie's blondeness seemed to be blinding in the sunlight. Or was it that her blondeness made Dena's darkness more conspicuous?

It was not until they got in their class line that anyone remembered to look for Theresa. Jonathan scolded her teasingly about her quietness. "Why don't you girls take a lesson from Tweedy. She's what my mother calls a good listener. And *that,* my mother says, will make you the most popular person in the world."

Theresa flushed. Jonathan was looking at her as if he thought her pretty special. Boys usually went by her without seeing her at all.

When Kenneth came in the line, everyone crowded around him with their questions. He had not been punished. Mrs. Jennet believed him when he said he had not made the nasty crack and did not know who had.

Theresa watched for the teacher in charge to come over to the line. She sighed with relief when the buzzer sounded and everyone popped into place.

In class Mrs. Jennet appointed Julie to be Theresa's buddy. Julie was to explain about the class science fair and help Theresa decide on a suitable topic.

Julie giggled. "Someone will have to help me get one first," she said. The science fair was several weeks away. Mrs. Jennet wanted each person to select a subject or an experiment and to report to her for approval.

"We have until Friday," Julie said. "Everything is happening on Friday, it seems." Friday was the day the club met and on this Friday the club director was going to begin casting the operetta.

Casually Julie asked Theresa if she were going to join the club. "We need a big chorus, you could be in that even if you're not a good singer."

Usually teachers chose the children with loud voices. She had always been the one to pull the curtains and to help make the scenery. She did not want to join any club especially since Mrs. Chinton did not like the club. "No, thanks, I don't like plays," Theresa said abruptly.

"Needn't be snippy," Julie said with no hard feelings. "I just wanted you to know that you're welcome to join if you like." She told Theresa about the topics for the science fair—how electricity serves us; living things and what makes them grow; weather and how we predict it, and a few other topics. Julie seemed disinterested in all of them.

"I hate science," she said mildly as she led Theresa to the back of the room where their reading group was to meet for a lesson.

The class was divided into three groups. Jonathan and

Dena were in the top group. Mrs. Jennet was in front of the room with them. They had their chairs arranged in a semi-circle near the board. Mrs. Jennet, sitting at the end of the semi-circle, could see the entire room.

A middle group of readers were in their own places. Bert and Kenneth were in that group. They were working by themselves on a phonics lesson in their phonics textbooks.

Theresa's group, the bottom one, was also in a semi-circle. They were partly facing the windows and they were doing a workbook assignment until Mrs. Jennet was ready to read with them. Theresa was in a good position to see and hear everyone in the room.

Jonathan's group was answering questions about a story they had read. Dena never seemed to have to think about an answer. Her answers came out almost before the question was completed. Theresa listened to Jonathan's voice each time he was called on. She liked the slow way he talked.

Theresa was glad when the first day of school was over. She had not learned much, but she felt she had survived. On the way home they were all busy talking about Bert and his nastiness, Bob and Kenneth's desire to "knock sense in Bert's head," and the operetta.

The girls had one other topic of conversation: how to get Hattie to tidy up her appearance.

"If I were any good at fixing hair I'd pull her into the girls' room and give her hair a good brushing," Dena said.

Julie said that if anyone brought a hairbrush she would gladly braid Hattie's hair neatly and pull it back in the style that Tweedy wore hers . . . Then they looked for Theresa and pulled her into the group so that Dena could see how her hair was worn.

Hair talk and clothes talk was the kind of talk Theresa was used to. She had no trouble saying a word or two when she was directly spoken to. Julie was all for helping Hattie instead of complaining about her.

"Can anyone sew? Has anyone got a button?" she asked, looking at Dena, Jennie, and Theresa in turn.

"I guess I can," Theresa said hesitantly. She did not think Mrs. Chinton would mind if she took a needle and thread to school. Buttons were always easy to get in a house where people sewed. Yet she did not like the idea of butting into anyone's business. Hattie's dress was Hattie's affair.

Julie took her answer as positive and when Dena said she could wash an old hairbrush of hers and bring it to school, Julie made plans to ask Mrs. Jennet for permission to spend the next recess in the girls' room with Hattie.

"If I had a robe to fit her I'd even get her dress washed. You could hang it over the radiator, Tweedy, while I . . ."

Theresa did not wait to hear the rest of the plan. She slipped off the path and began hurrying toward her building on the grass. Jonathan reached her first.

"Say, what scared you? I saw you getting along just great with the girls. Somebody say something to hurt you?"

Julie came next. "Wow, you went fast. Did I do something wrong?"

Julie's blue eyes reminded Theresa of Miss Wilner's. They had the same gentle quality. Miss Wilner! Gosh, she had forgotten her promise.

"I can't be butting into anybody's business," she said bluntly.

Julie giggled. "Why didn't you say so right away?" They waited for Dena and Jennie to join them. When they were all together on the path, Julie said, "Tweedy has a point. I'm stupid. Maybe Hattie won't want us fixing her up."

"We'll make her want it. She makes me ashamed to be black every time I look at her." Dena opened her eyes wide and looked more frog-like than ever.

Jennie suggested that Julie ask Hattie before they made further plans. She offered to bring an old dress of hers so that the girls could do a good sewing and washing job on the one Hattie was wearing.

Theresa walked with the girls. Once again Miss Wilner's advice had been helpful. The girls complimented her on her common sense and Jonathan was smiling at her.

At home she was able to tell Mrs. Chinton about Hattie and the plans the girls were making to help the girl. Mrs. Chinton thought it a fine idea for the Negro girls in the class to stick by each other.

When homework and the science project were discussed, Mrs. Chinton suggested that Theresa might try to think of something with sewing or cooking in it since she did well in those areas.

Conscientiously, Theresa did as her foster mother told her to do. She thought of the sewing machine parts and tried to find pictures of how they went together. Using an electric sewing machine was much easier than understanding how it worked. She gave up on it.

Cooking seemed to have no science angle she could latch on to for the project. When her foster father was consulted he examined the list of topics and pursed his lips.

"Living things . . . Now what around here could be considered in that category?" His eyes roved around the room. Theresa's eyes followed his.

"Plants," she cried as she saw the window boxes outside on the terrace. "Can I do something about plants?"

After dinner she sat in the living room skimming through a plant book. There was an entire section on transplanting plants. Mr. Chinton helped her read the chapter and explained the big words. "Isn't this what you did with my ivy?" she asked.

It was. Slowly, with Mr. Chinton's help, she wrote part of what she had learned. Good soil for ivy had to be neither acid nor alkaline. "What would happen if I had used plain sand in my transplant?" Theresa asked. "Or acid soil?".

"You might try to find out," Mr. Chinton said. "That would make a fine experiment. You have your ivy planted in good soil. Now we can buy another ivy like yours and transplant a snip in another kind of soil."

"Then I can feed them the same way and watch them and see which grows better."

Mrs. Chinton nodded. "Only for a science project you would have to measure and keep accurate records of exactly what you do and what you feed your plant."

Theresa had meant to write to Laura Gardiner that night to tell her about her new class, but somehow the

evening went too fast. Homework took hours and then she began thinking about her experiment.

My mother would like that project, she thought as she adjusted her plant a fraction of an inch on its shelf. In a way, her mother was helping her to do it.

Her dreams that night were mostly friendly ones, with Jonathan chasing Bert all around the topsoil hill playing a guitar and singing while he did so.

Mrs. Jennet liked the experiment that Theresa planned. She asked Theresa about the kind of soil she was to use and how she would know it was acid. On the board Theresa had to write the words litmus paper, alkaline, and acid. Theresa was glad she had copied the words right out of the book.

Several children raised their hands. "Could I do an experiment like that?" Paul asked.

"Me, too. Me, too," another child called out.

Jonathan and Julie both passed Theresa a note asking if she had any more ivy so that they might work with plants, too.

Mrs. Jennet told Theresa that her experiment might be made broader. Julie nudged Theresa. "Please think of something for me. I'm so stupid in science."

"Will you help the people who wish to do something with plants?" Mrs. Jennet asked Theresa.

"Help in science?" Theresa gulped. She had never been able to help anyone in schoolwork. Now people were begging her for ideas. To her amazement an idea was coming to her mind.

"Maybe—maybe we could use different soils . . . like

Julie could use an alkaline one . . . and . . . and Jonathan could use sand . . . and somebody . . . maybe Paul, could put his plant too deep and . . ."

I'm doing it, Theresa was saying to herself. *I'm talking and the class is listening. Golly, is this me?*

She went on giving possibilities until every idea she had read in the book had been told. Then she sat down, and marveled at herself.

Eleven

That first week was a busy one for Theresa. Mrs. Chinton made her do lots of studying after her homework was finished. In class, she helped several people to begin their transplanting. Dena convinced all the other children doing the transplanting to come to Friday afternoon's club tryouts. Theresa was the only one to refuse.

At home she finished her blouse and began her jumper. Mrs. Chinton complimented her for the neat way she tied off her beginning and end stitches. Calling her "Mother" was almost easy now.

With Mrs. Chinton's help, Theresa lengthened her old dress and laundered it. "Slip it into Hattie's desk when no one is looking," Mrs. Chinton advised.

Hattie had accepted the dress and had worn it the next day. She thanked Theresa.

"Show me how to sew on a button. When I sew one on it comes off right away," Hattie had said.

Theresa brought a needle and thread and a button to school and showed Hattie how to double her thread, make neat stitches, and finish the sewing so that the thread would not come untied.

Julie took Hattie into the girls' room to talk with her. She did not tell anyone what was said, but Theresa could guess because the next day Hattie came in looking well scrubbed. She also brought a comb and brush with her.

"Can you help me comb my hair like yours?" Hattie looked at Theresa with pleading eyes.

Theresa put her hand up to her hair. "You mean this funny old braid? And a pony tail? That's easy."

It was during recess and Mrs. Jennet let the girls go out to the girls' room to help restyle Hattie's hair. She was pleased.

"I like to see girls helping each other to look neat and pretty," she said when they returned. "I'm glad to see Theresa coming out of her shell a bit, too," she added.

When Theresa told Mrs. Chinton what Mrs. Jennet had said, Mrs. Chinton laughed. "Working together is the best way for children to get friendly. I'm glad you're making friends already."

Mrs. Chinton was still worrying about "the wild boys" she saw around the cooperative when school was out. She called the school and the co-op management office to complain about the topsoil hill.

"If you see any boys fighting or throwing things, keep far away and come right home," Mrs. Chinton reminded Theresa each day. "Black children need to learn to run fast."

"Miss Wilner told me not to run," Theresa said.

Mrs. Chinton laughed merrily. "Don't run from Dad or me . . . only run from people who will hurt you."

Theresa promised to do that. "Running is the thing I find easiest to do," she said with a giggle.

In her conversations with Mrs. Chinton, the only bit of truth about her classmates Theresa omitted telling was the color of their skin. She knew that Mrs. Chinton assumed that Jennie, Paul, and Julie were black. About Jonathan, Theresa said little. He was one of the "wild" boys Mrs. Chinton had warned her to stay away from.

When Mr. Chinton came home from work on Friday, he asked, "Mother, do you think that Theresa should join the Junior Civic Club? One of the men who lives in section four thought that she might enjoy meeting new friends."

"I don't want to join any club," Theresa said before her foster mother could answer. "Anyway, there are white kids in it. I know. Some are in my class." She looked toward Mrs. Chinton for approval.

Mrs. Chinton smiled. "I know all about that club. Weeks ago, I heard some of our white neighbors talking about it. And since then I've listened to the ladies in the laundry room. No, Dad. I do not think that this club is the place for our little girl."

Mr. Chinton looked disappointed as he continued. "This man thinks all of us ought to join to support the club because a few fresh white boys are tearing up the posters and threatening to disrupt the club meetings and rehearsals."

"Bert and his Dukes," Theresa said without thinking.

When Mrs. Chinton had wormed that story out of Theresa, she was more positive than ever that Theresa should keep away from the club.

Mr. Chinton argued for a while. He said he thought he might attend the next adult meeting. "I want to put my word in about the outside community," he said. "The cooperative must be convinced that children and adults from across the boulevard should be welcomed to the community center clubs."

When Mrs. Chinton complained that the talk was making her head ache, Mr. Chinton began his gardening chores. Theresa was happy to have quiet in the house again.

She went to her room and measured her ivy. It had grown half an inch and it was sturdy and bright-looking. Gazing at it brought her real mother very close.

"We've both changed since we came here," she whispered. She busied herself measuring and recording the changes in the second ivy plant in her science project transplant.

They were eating dinner when Theresa heard singing coming from the path that ran from the community center to their circle. She could see the path from the window. Five boys and girls were walking along and singing a song about making the punishment fit the crime.

"That's a song from the *Mikado*," Mr. Chinton said.

"I guess those children are coming home from the club meeting." He said no more. Theresa kept her face blank. She did not want to show that she had recognized Jonathan's clear tenor voice.

She ate her chop and strained to hear the last faint sound of the song, but she allowed herself no tears. If Mrs. Chinton did not like the club, then she did not want any part of it. It would be fun but she didn't want to cause any trouble at home.

After dinner she worked on her jumper while Mrs. Chinton began cutting fabric for two shirts to keep Theresa company. They would be gifts for each of the boys. The sewing machine was pulled into the kitchen to keep threads off the rug, and Mr. Chinton turned on the television.

Theresa and Mrs. Chinton talked about the sewing and about the boys. Theresa could listen endlessly to stories about her foster brothers.

When it was time for the machine to be rolled back into the bedroom, Mr. Chinton had altogether regained his good humor. He tweaked Theresa's braid playfully and said, "Guess I shouldn't worry about your being lonely. You look happy enough chit-chatting with your mother. Girls are not like boys. Maybe they don't *need* kids their age the same as boys do."

"I see plenty of kids in school," Theresa reminded him. "And I want to keep out of trouble. I've got plenty to do at home, don't I, Mother?"

Mrs. Chinton hugged her, and Theresa was glad she had talked up. This was how she liked her foster parents to look at her and each other. While all the talk about the club had been going on, they had been frowning and unhappy.

She put her hand in Mr. Chinton's. He pressed it and walked with her to her room.

The next day was Saturday. After Theresa helped vacuum the apartment, she went out for a brisk walk with Mr. Chinton.

Mr. Chinton laughed when he saw Theresa dressed in jeans. "With your hair hidden under your hat, you look like a boy," he said.

Mrs. Chinton wound a scarf around Theresa's neck. "Not a bit like a boy. She looks delicious. Good enough to eat."

"Dainty?" Theresa asked. That was what Jonathan had called her.

"Dainty indeed," both grown-ups answered.

Theresa went out of the apartment humming. She walked with her foster father, matching step for step. The wind was strong, but she did not mind it. Her coat was warm and the scarf hid part of her face.

Not many children were out, and those who could be seen were mostly on bicycles, riding swiftly past the walkers. It was not until they were on the path leading from the school to their house that Theresa recognized anyone she knew.

Even from a distance she knew the broad-shouldered boy who swaggered. She grabbed Mr. Chinton's hand.

"What's wrong? What made you jump?"

"Nothing. Mother told me to watch out for wild boys and I think I see some." She went to the other side of the path.

"You mean those boys on the topsoil hill?"

Theresa nodded. Mr. Chinton raised his brows. "I've seen those boys around. They're the ones who are pulling down the club signs and making threats. I don't blame Mother for warning you about *them*."

From behind her foster father's back, Theresa peered at the boys riding down the topsoil hill. Bert was clearly visible. His brown hair fell over his forehead and eyes; his smile was cold but his brown eyes were even colder. He faced Theresa, his bicycle beside him. He pushed the bike up the side of the hill.

"Bet you can't ride down without hands," a boy dared him.

"Bet I can," Bert shouted back.

"Bert can do *anything*," another voice cried out. "He's a DUKE. DUKES CAN DO ANYTHING!"

Mr. Chinton clicked his tongue against his teeth. "Tch. Tch. Tch. Coming down that hill on a bike without using hands is dangerous. Fool boys, to dare him, and he's an even bigger fool to take the dare." He quickened his step.

Bert was on top of the hill now. He whooped and cried, "Watch me."

"Stop that!" Mr. Chinton's voice resounded through the parking lot.

Bert looked down. "Talking to me, mister?"

"Yes. Don't you think riding your bike down that steep hill is dangerous enough with both hands on the handle bars?"

Theresa kept her face hidden. She did not like the sneer on Bert's face. She did not like the way Bert's friends were looking at Bert expectantly, encouraging him to be clever.

"The only danger about it is for YOU," Bert yelled as he put his leg over the side of the bicycle. "Because if you don't get out of the way fast, *you might get hurt.*"

His laughter, and the laughter of the other boys made Theresa whimper, "Let's go, Dad. Let's go, please."

Mr. Chinton, after a long look at Bert, turned away. He was breathing heavily as they walked away from the hill where Bert crazily rode down with his hands up in the air.

"Who said I couldn't do it?" Bert screamed. "Who said?"

"Who can't do that?" asked another voice.

Theresa whirled around to see who had ridden up from the boulevard side of the hill. The voice was familiar. So was the next voice, which cried,

"Watch us do it . . ."

Bob and Kenneth were riding toward the hill together. Behind them came other bicycles in a single line. When Bob and Kenneth dismounted, they began pushing their bikes up the hill.

The white boys ran to the top of the mound. "Keep off. This is our property," Bert yelled.

"We were here before you were born," Bob shouted and continued pushing his bicycle upward.

"Theresa," Mr. Chinton said when they passed the parking lot, "I want you to go right home. I'm afraid there is going to be trouble. I don't like the sound of this. You go home and tell Mother I'll be up in a minute."

"I want to call a policeman," he said. "Before someone gets hurt." Before he turned into the mall, he called, "Don't say anything to Mother about this. She's frightened enough as is."

Theresa watched him disappear into the enclosed shopping center. Then she set her feet on the path leading to their building.

"Keep moving," she told herself. "Don't look back."

But her steps grew shorter and shorter. The voices from behind her kept ringing in her ears. Something made her want to see what was happening. She was frightened and attracted at the same time.

Bert's voice rang out. "I dare you to come up here and ride down the way I did. I *dare* you!"

"Here I come."

Theresa stepped backward. She turned so that she could see the hill. Her heart was beating double time.

All the white boys were on one side of the hill. All the Negro boys were on the other. Bert was on top of the hill holding onto his bicycle. Kenneth was halfway up, pushing his bike steadily.

"Give him a chance," Bert was saying with a mocking laugh. "Let the ape come up and break his neck riding down."

Bob cried out, "Kenny, come on down. Don't go up there. He's going to play dirty . . ."

"Hear that? Why don't you listen to your friend?" Bert jeered.

Steadily Kenneth walked up the hill. Theresa could not catch her breath. She heard the boys calling each other names. But she paid no attention to the insults. All that mattered was the boy on top of the hill and the boy almost level with him.

The white boy and the black boy stood side by side. Kenneth's face was set; Bert's was taunting.

Theresa did not want to see any more. She began to walk quickly in the direction of home, when from behind her a rock came flying. She turned to see who had hit her and almost at once she was pelted with another stone.

She jumped behind a bench and hid there, trembling. The rocks were not being thrown at her. They were being thrown at the Negro boys by the whites.

Now the stones were being hurled in both directions. Threats and insults went with them. Theresa did not dare move. She put her hand on her cheek where the second rock had hit her.

Her hand came away with a spot of blood. She was staring at her reddened palm when she heard Kenneth's voice ring out.

"Out of my way, I'm coming down," he yelled.

"Don't, Kenny," Bob called to him from behind a car.

"Don't, Ken-ny," mocked Bert.

"Out of my way." Kenneth gave himself one big push and rose high on his bicycle.

The rocks stopped falling. There was a hush. With one loud whoop, Kenneth began coming down the hill, hands outstretched at his side.

Almost at once the white boys cleared a path for him. He was halfway down, then three quarters. One eighth of the way to go when Bert shoved his bike from the top of the hill at Kenneth. Kenneth swerved to avoid the en-

tangling wheels. His bicycle came to a dead stop, and he tumbled over his own handle bars. He landed on Bert's bicycle, his own bike twisted around his legs.

"No!" Theresa screamed as she saw him fall. "No," she screamed as she saw the boys jumping on their bicycles and riding away.

White boys and black boys disappeared, leaving Kenneth lying there on the hill. *Cops will come,* Theresa thought. They always came after a fight in Harlem. She ought to run.

Run, Theresa told herself. But her legs would not budge. She touched her bloody cheek and stared at Kenneth's still body.

You always *run away,* Theresa reminded herself. But she was not running away now.

In the instant it took her to get to Kenneth, she thought of Miss Wilner and the Chintons. They had helped her when she needed help.

"I've got to stay with you. You can't be left alone," she wailed as she gathered Kenneth's bruised head in her arms gently. "Nobody should be left alone. Nobody."

Twelve

" . . . To make the punishment fit the crime, the punishment fit the crime . . ."

Theresa recognized the song from the *Mikado* and looked around to see where the singers were. She saw them coming from the third circle of buildings.

"Jonny! Julie!" she called.

Her voice came out cracked and hoarse. She did not think it could be heard. She tried to move Kenneth's head from where it lay on her lap so she could wave.

"Ouch," Kenneth groaned.

"Kenny, are you all right?" Theresa wiped his face with her fingertips.

Kenneth tried to sit up and fell back at once. "My leg," he cried.

Theresa was so happy to hear his voice that she called out clearly, "Jonny! Julie! Hey, come here!"

The song stopped abruptly. She heard Jonathan call her name and in a few seconds she was surrounded by her friends.

While they were asking her what had happened to Kenneth and how she got the bruise on her face, they heard sirens. "Cops and an ambulance coming into the parking lot," Jonathan announced. "They'll get these bikes off you in no time, Ken."

A woman came into the circle just before the doctor arrived. Jonathan introduced her to Theresa as "Mrs. Shinerman." Julie called the woman, "Mother." Theresa knew Julie's name was Fisher, but she was too upset to think about it.

While the doctor and the policeman disentangled Kenneth from the bicycles, Mrs. Shinerman examined Theresa's cut.

"Nothing serious," she said. The policeman checked over Theresa and discharged her in the care of Mr. Chinton, who by this time had returned with the policeman who was on duty in the mall shopping center.

Julie had been listening to the report Theresa made to the policeman. She heard Mr. Chinton give his name and address. While Jonathan and Paul and Bob, who had returned, gave the policeman Bert's name and the names of some of the other boys in Bert's group, Julie slipped over to Theresa and whispered, "I'm a foster child. Are you? I heard your father say his name is Chinton and I know your name is Ellmsby; it comes right before mine when Mrs. Jennet calls the role."

Theresa forgot about her cut face. She forgot about the crowd. "Are you one? For real?"

When Julie nodded solemnly, Theresa felt her heart go out to the white girl. To be a foster child and also have to wear those awful braces on her teeth seemed more than any one person ought to have to bear! She put out her hand toward Julie's.

Julie squeezed it hard. "Is your family nice? Mine is super."

While Theresa was telling Julie about Donald and Fred, Jonathan and the others joined the two girls. Theresa glanced up to see Mr. Chinton and Mrs. Shinerman talking to the policeman from the shopping center. The ambulance had already left, taking Kenneth to the hospital. The police car had gone off to get Kenneth's parents.

Jonathan interrupted the conversation just as Julie was telling Theresa how much she loved her little brother.

Jonathan chuckled. "She ought to love Timmy," he said. "If it wasn't for Timmy deciding to take a nap in the playground she wouldn't have made friends with me . . ."

Dena scolded Jonathan for making fun at a time like this, but Jonathan refused to stop his story. Paul and Julie said that since Kenneth had only a broken leg, Dena need not act as if he were dead or dying. They helped Jonathan tell the story of how Julie met Jonathan and them.

"It's got something to do with this fight," Julie said. "Because soon after our family moved into this circle there was a fight. What we didn't know that day was that all of us who were fighting with one another would soon be friends and acting together in an operetta."

The story was complicated, but with Dena's help Theresa finally understood what had happened. The first week Julie had lived in the cooperative, she had come down with Timmy to the playground. She had stood around watching the boys and girls taking turns on a strange-looking slide.

Timmy had fallen asleep and she pushed the carriage under a tree and climbed on the slide. Immediately she realized that there was a quiet struggle going on. From the distance, she had not noticed that when the white children were on the slide, all the Negro children stayed off.

"I'm so used to all kinds of kids that I don't see colors any more," Julie confessed in embarrassment. "In the shelter where I lived for a long time, we had all kinds of kids. And we always stuck together. The "ins" against the "outs.""

Now, "in" was the cooperative, instead of the shelter, Dena explained. That day Julie had sided with some of the more stubborn white children who wanted the black children to leave the playground. The Negro children, except for Jonathan, lived across the boulevard and had come into the playground to see the new slide.

The white children, some of the ones who now called themselves the Dukes, began to chase the Negro children off the slide. Paul and Jennie and several others had run up to their apartments to tell their mothers that a fight was brewing. But most of the children had remained, Julie among them.

"You don't belong here. The playground is for the kids who live here," she had screamed at a girl who was climbing the slide. Up she had run ahead of the girl, squeezing past her on the steps.

Jonathan smiled at Theresa. " 'Cept for you, she's the skinniest kid I ever saw. That's what made the accident."

He had been siding with the Negro children, feeling more a part of the outside community than of the cooperative. He had climbed up the slide from the side and had pushed Julie just as she had settled herself across the top of the slide in order to prevent anyone else from going down.

"I didn't expect her to weigh less than a feather," Jonathan said. "Was I surprised to see her go flying off the slide."

She had landed on the pavement, face first. Jonathan had taken her upstairs with a trail of children pushing the baby carriage.

"And she never blamed me," Jonathan said. "And when her social worker, Miss Wilner, came and I told her the truth, Julie kept saying it was her fault."

"Miss Wilner?"

Theresa remembered, Miss Wilner's other client. It had been Julie . . . Julie suddenly became more than a friend. They shared Miss Wilner as well as foster families. She wanted to tell Julie, but Jonathan and Dena were having an argument about Bert.

Dena was saying that Julie's accident and Kenneth's

had nothing in common, that Julie and Bert had nothing in common.

"Maybe Bert will get to be friends. Maybe he'll be so sorry, like Julie was sorry, and maybe we can even get him to be Ko-Ko in our show. He'd be a good executioner, that is all I can say," Paul ended.

Dena objected to the idea of having Bert in their show. "Julie knew black kids and she wasn't prejudiced. Bert never will get to know what we're like, so don't do any dreaming about his changing." She took a pile of leaflets from a bench. The others picked up theirs from under the rock they had used to weigh the leaflets down.

Almost apologetically, the group explained that they had been putting the leaflets under doors in the various buildings. They had had a meeting on Friday, and during the tryouts Jonathan had gotten the part of Nanki-Poo, the prince, Julie had gotten the part of Yum-Yum, and Dena was Katisha.

"I had no competition," Dena said wryly. "Nobody else wanted to be the ugly girl that Nanki-Poo runs away from."

"And I'm the Mikado," Paul said proudly.

"I heard you singing last night when you came home," Theresa said with a tinge of envy in her voice. "The songs sound very nice."

"Especially the Mikado's song," Jennie began to sing, ". . . make the punishment fit the crime."

"I'd like to find the right punishment for Bert . . . ," Jonathan muttered.

Julie flushed. "Don't talk like that. You keep out of it. Your father will not let you take part in the operetta if you get into any more fights."

Jonathan balled up a leaflet and threw it across the path into a litter basket. "Who says I'm going to fight. All I said is that I wished I knew a punishment for Bert and his crew."

Jonathan walked away with Paul, complaining that he never was able to satisfy girls. Dena objected when he thought Bert could change, and Julie objected when he wondered about punishments.

By this time Theresa had lost the opportunity to ask Julie about Miss Wilner. Mr. Chinton and Mrs. Shinerman were walking toward them; they were ready to go home. The policeman had all the information he needed.

Julie untwined her fingers from Theresa's. And Mr. Chinton put his arm under Theresa's. Mr. Chinton talked to Mrs. Shinerman as their small party moved toward their circle of houses. Mrs. Shinerman was asking him to join the adult club and he was explaining why he could not.

"I'm worried, too," Mrs. Shinerman said. "I can sympathize with your wife. If the fights become more violent, I will move, too."

"Oh, no, Mom!" Julie cried. "I don't want to move. I've never in all my life been in a real club and in an operetta with costumes and everything. Please don't move, Mom."

Theresa leaned toward Julie. She thought of Julie going back to the shelter. How sad for Julie if once again she were sent back there, when at last she had a home.

Her own situation seemed mild compared with Julie's. It was as much for Julie's sake as it was for her own that she nudged her friend and made her listen to Mr. Chinton say, "Let's hope someone can find a way to stop the violence before it really builds up. Let's do more than hope so."

"Julie," Theresa whispered. "Ask him to try to find a way. He found a way to save my ivy and it was half dead. He's good at saving things."

Julie asked and Mr. Chinton said he would devote his thoughts to the subject and when he had an idea he would share it with the adult club and anyone else who was interested.

"Julie and Jonny tell me that we really owe quite a few of our new members to Theresa," Mrs. Shinerman said as they waited together for the elevators. "It was through her science project that the children got together. Too bad Theresa can't join."

"When Mrs. Chinton gets more confidence in this community, we'll see about Theresa's joining," Mr. Chinton promised. "Right now we have to find a way to get Theresa and her cut face into the house without her mother fainting."

Mrs. Chinton did not faint when she saw Theresa's face. "I expected trouble," she said and hurriedly took Theresa into the bathroom to wash the cut with soap and water.

"I'm fine," Theresa kept saying, but her foster mother kept cleaning the wound until she was sure that no infection could set in.

"I'll set the table for dinner now," Theresa said.

The door bell rang just as the glasses were being put on the table. Mr. Chinton went to the door. Theresa listened—visitors were extremely rare. Her first thought was that the police had come back to get her. She held on to the table until she heard Mr. Chinton say, "Come in, ladies."

A strange voice apologized for disturbing them at this hour. "Only the seriousness of the problem would make me leave my family and come out before dinner was served," the strange woman said.

Theresa saw a tall lady walk toward the kitchen door. Behind her was Mrs. Shinerman. Theresa smiled to her and received a smile in return.

"Marjorie, these ladies want to speak to you for a moment." Mr. Chinton stuck his head into the kitchen.

Theresa saw her foster mother step behind the kitchen cabinets. "I'm serving dinner now," she said curtly.

"Our *visitors* have something to ask you . . ."

"Me? What could they have to ask me that you can't answer?" Mrs. Chinton turned the water on in the sink.

Please, don't let her be rude, Theresa whispered to herself.

Mrs. Chinton shut off the water. She dried her hands. Theresa stayed behind her foster mother as she walked into the living room.

The tall woman with Mrs. Shinerman was Mrs. Thompson, Jonathan's mother. She was pretty and had a soft voice. Mrs. Chinton said hello to her without looking at Mrs. Shinerman.

Mrs. Shinerman immediately began talking about the meeting that was just held in the Toler house. Mrs. Chinton said she was not interested in the problems of the cooperative. "If decent people can't live here in peace, then we'll have to move out of here," she said.

Theresa was ashamed for her foster mother. Mrs. Shinerman's soft brown eyes had grown cloudy as if with tears. Mrs. Chinton was acting as if Mrs. Shinerman were not even in the room.

Mrs. Chinton was talking stiffly to Mrs. Thompson. Her face never turned toward the white woman. Mr. Chinton began talking to Mrs. Shinerman as if to hide his wife's behavior.

He explained to Mrs. Shinerman that people in the building had embarrassed Mrs. Chinton by asking her if she knew any cleaning ladies. "And when I come into the elevator at night and someone is riding with me, I feel them staring at me, wondering if I'm a thief or a mugger," he said. "So I don't blame her for the way she feels."

Mrs. Shinerman sighed. "I know that some people are afraid of Negroes. But how will they ever learn not to be frightened if people move away. A cooperative is a small village—we all own our own homes. We should be here to stay."

Mrs. Thompson and Mrs. Shinerman did not stay long. They could not convince Mrs. Chinton to join the civic club, or give a contribution toward a large meeting in the community center.

"If you don't want to work with us to stop the fights, you may still want to join us for social reasons," Mrs. Thompson said before she left. "We have speakers at our meetings and serve refreshments."

When Mrs. Chinton showed no interest in meetings or speakers, Mrs. Thompson smiled sadly. "Perhaps you'll let your daughter join the junior club. I understand she sews well and is friendly with many of the club members. We could use her talents in our forthcoming operetta."

"Theresa, today, has had a sample of integrated fun," Mrs. Chinton snapped. "No thank you, I'll keep my daughter at home, where she'll be safe."

Mr. Chinton whispered to Theresa after the visitors were gone, "Don't get discouraged, Theresa. Give me time. I'll find some way to convince Mother. I made up my mind about that when we moved here. I'd hoped that having a child in the house would make her friendlier toward the neighbors." He hugged Theresa and said, "It's too soon to see any changes. I'm sure that your presence here will work the miracle . . . I'm sure of it."

In bed that night, Theresa pulled Mrs. Chinton closer. "Mother, Miss Wilner says that it's wrong to run away when you're scared. She told me to hang around for a while to find out if I've got a good reason to be scared."

"I understand, child. She's a smart woman, Miss Wilner is, but I've hung around white people long enough to *know* they're dangerous." She stroked Theresa's cheek. "Don't you worry none, child. A sweet girl like you shouldn't have to worry, ever."

Her window was open slightly. She heard singing coming from another window. The message seemed as if it were meant especially for her. "We shall o-ver-come-m-m. We shall over come-m," she hummed as she fell asleep. *Don't worry, Julie . . . Be like me. Don't worry . . . We shall overcome.*

Thirteen

On Monday morning her confidence was high. As she had done on every other morning since she had been with the Chintons, she made her bed and checked to see if her plants needed water. Then she put a stamp on the short letter she had written to her foster brothers last evening.

"I'm going," she called to Mrs. Chinton, and received the inevitable and comforting reply, "Have a good morning, Theresa."

Down near the elevator she found Julie and Jonathan. Both looked upset. Theresa softly said, "Don't worry, Julie. I'm sure we'll find some way to stop the fighting . . ."

"Then we better start finding that way right now," Julie declared. She unfolded the paper Jonathan held in his hand. "Look at this."

A skull and crossbones were drawn on top of the page. Under the picture, in capitals, was printed:

BROKEN HEADS HURT MORE THAN BROKEN LEGS.

IF YOU DON'T WANT A BROKEN HEAD,

YOU BETTER KEEP AWAY

FROM THE APES THAT DON'T BELONG HERE.

"Dena got one of them, too," Julie said. "They were shoved under the doors early this morning. How do you like that?"

They met Dena who had gone to call for Jennie in the next building. Jennie was furious at Bert. Dena refused to let her anger get the best of her.

"This is too serious to feel angry. My mother wants to take my letter to the police."

Jonathan answered, "What can the police do?"

"We must stop this kind of threat and this kind of talk," Dena replied.

Paul, when he met them, agreed with her. "But how?" he asked.

"A committee is going to visit Bert's family," Dena said. "When they talk about Kenneth, they can discuss this, too."

"But what if Bert says he didn't write the letters?"

Everyone looked at Paul. He had no answer.

"Then we have to tell all the kids to run when they see Bert or his gang coming. We've got to be good runners," Jennie said.

"People will begin moving if there's trouble," Julie said softly and pressed Theresa's hand. "I guess we'll just have to learn to run if we don't want any more broken legs."

"Miss Wilner told me not to run." Theresa looked into Julie's blue eyes and stopped talking. She wondered if during the night Julie had envisioned herself back in the shelter. "Miss Wilner told me . . ." she repeated in confusion.

"Miss Wilner?" All eyes were on Theresa. "Is that Julie's Miss Wilner?"

Everyone had met Miss Wilner after Julie's accident. They thought her great. Jonathan had also met Mr. Dyson when he had insisted on paying for part of the expensive braces.

Julie told the group that Mrs. Chinton might move away and leave Theresa homeless. "We have to stop all fighting," she said. "For Tweedy's sake."

Theresa wanted to hug the white girl. Julie was talking about her problem without even mentioning the fact that Mrs. Shinerman might move, too. She felt closer to Julie than she had to anyone, even Laura Gardiner. "I'd do anything for Julie," she said to herself. "Anything."

They came into the school yard laughing over the coincidence of Theresa and Julie being foster children, having the same social worker, and sharing a desk in the same class. "Almost twins," Jonathan said as the group entered the yard for lineup.

But the classes were scattered in strange places. Most of the Negro children seemed to be on the left side of the yard; most of the white kids on the right. The teacher

on duty was talking to Bert and another white boy.

From the left, Sharon waved. "Come over here."

"The teacher caught Bert calling me a name," Hattie told them when they joined the large group. "She's talking to him about it."

Sharon tossed her head. "We're going to do more than talk about it. Are you guys going to be with us? Or against us?"

Bob had Jonathan in a corner. Paul and Jennie were on the outside of the circle that had formed around Hattie and Sharon.

The report was that Bert had challenged the boys from across the boulevard to a fight. "This afternoon after school," Sharon said. "And we've accepted the challenge. After lunch all of us are going to the Field Street parking lot, which is across the street from the cooperative and under the railroad station. We're going to load up with ammunition and we want to know who's with us."

Theresa's palms grew moist. Julie pulled her back. From Dena came the only answer.

"Our parents don't want us to fight. My mother says that fighting never solves anything."

Julie was about to speak when Sharon shook her head. "We don't expect any whiteys to be with us, but we do expect everybody else to."

Theresa touched Julie gently. Julie was ready to cry. Together they moved back near Jennie and Paul. In the corner, Theresa saw a number of boys gathered. They were talking in loud whispers.

"You're chicken, Jonny. That's what you are. Chicken." Bob was glaring at Jonathan. A boy from an-

other class put up his fist and asked, "Do you think running away will save you? Like fun it will. My brother says that first Bert will kick *us* off the property and *then* he'll work over the few of you who live inside it. So get ready to fight. It'll be now *with us* or later *alone*."

Jonathan looked miserable. "It's not just for me I can't fight. It's for somebody else. My father says if I get into any more trouble, I'll lose my allowance."

Julie edged toward Jonathan. "It's for me," she explained to Theresa. "He's paying for part of my braces and if his father stops his allowance then he'll have to sell his guitar to pay his share."

Paul cleared his throat. "I don't know if I ought to tell you . . . but Jonny called Miss Wilner and asked if she could take you to the dentist just before the operetta." He told the girls that Jonathan wanted the braces removed for the performance. He was going to pay the extra expenses for the trip.

Julie knew all about it. She had agreed to be Yum-Yum only on that condition. "Bob," Julie said. "Don't nag Jonny. He can't fight. He told you that he's going to pay the dentist so that I can be in the operetta without my braces. He's not scared. He's just keeping his promise."

"That's good for you," Bob snapped. "For us it's nothing. We fight Bert and the Dukes at three-thirty today." He pointed to the white boys in a huddle across the yard from them. "See that. They stick together . . ."

"I'm not with them," Paul said.

"So what? Maybe you're chicken, too," Bob declared as the buzzer rang. "Meet us at three o'clock in the Field Street parking lot, or at three-thirty on the topsoil hill.

If you don't, you'll never have a friend again."

A teacher was nearby. Theresa saw Jonathan start to answer Bob and then change his mind. When the bell rang he got in line, silently. In class everybody told Mrs. Jennet about Kenneth's accident. Fingers pointed at Bert.

"I did not trip him," Bert cried. His face looked innocent. He looked around the room as if bewildered by the accusation. "We were fooling around and he fell. I fell, too."

Mrs. Jennet stopped the talk. She wrote arithmetic examples on the board and made everyone get to work.

That morning there was a great deal of mumbling in the room. Mrs. Jennet made the class put their books away and put their heads down on the table for five full minutes. But no sooner was the punishment over than the buzzing began again.

Notes were passed between Bert and his friends. Notes were passed among all the club members. Every time Mrs. Jennet tried to find the noisy ones, the class immediately became quiet so that she could not catch anyone.

Theresa could not keep her attention on her work. Even during the science period when she recorded her ivy's growth for the week, her mind was on the fight.

Julie did more erasing than writing that morning.

"If Jonny gets punished, then I'm not going to be in the operetta, either," she wrote to Theresa.

"Maybe he won't fight," Theresa answered. It was more prayer than hope. Bob had sent a note to all the Negro boys. When it had come back to him, he had nodded to Jonathan. That could mean only that Jonathan had agreed to fight.

Without meaning to peek, Theresa could not help seeing the doodles Julie made that morning. Whole pages of Japanese girls with umbrellas and black teeth! Each one was labeled, "Me!"

Theresa inched close to Julie. "I think you look pretty even with the braces. Honest."

Julie covered her mouth and grinned. "We better try to figure out a way to stop this fight. We better."

At lunchtime, Jonathan disappeared from the line. The girls walked home without him. All they talked about were ways to stop the fight.

Dena was for going to Bert's parents and to all the other white boys' parents. Julie wanted parents kept out.

Jennie thought that going to the Negro boys' homes might be better. "That won't be tattling because Bob and the other boys haven't done anything wrong yet."

No one liked that idea, either. Julie was going to call Mr. Dyson or Miss Wilner when she got home. Dena told her that social workers ate lunch too, and probably neither of them would be in the office.

Dena's deep voice reminded Theresa of Val Gardiner's. When Val was excited, her voice grew deep like Dena's.

"I know what to do!" Theresa exclaimed. "My friend Val once took Laura and me to a meeting. In a church. There was a big crowd and my mother came with us."

She recalled that long-forgotten Sunday afternoon. The minister had talked a lot about Dr. Martin Luther King, who had won a peace prize and later had been assassinated. All over the world, Val had said, people knew about Dr. King.

He had talked about the black people and how they ought to get together and march and make strikes. That had been the day she had learned to sing "We shall overcome."

"I know what we must do," Theresa said breathlessly. "We have to picket Bert. We have to make signs and march and sing."

"Aw, that's corny," Dena said. "How can we picket Bert?"

Julie's face had brightened. "Maybe we could think of a way . . . It would be swell if we could stop the fight. I don't want Jonny to get in trouble. I wish you could figure out a way, Tweedy. Try, will you?"

Theresa would have done anything for Julie at that moment. Julie was telling about the shelter she had been in. "Theresa will have to go to one. We don't want her to lose her good family, do we?" she asked.

Jennie sighed. "You're always sticking up for everybody. We all agree with you. What can we do?"

Dena tapped her foot. "Tweedy, think hard."

Julie nodded. "It'll help me, too. Because my foster mother will move away if there is trouble in the co-op. So let's all of us *think*." They went home to lunch thinking.

To all of Mrs. Chinton's questions about school, Theresa gave the same answer, "It was okay." To the questions about the children's reaction to Kenneth's accident, she said, "They didn't like it."

There had been an announcement about the topsoil hill over the loudspeaker in school and she told Mrs.

Chinton what the principal had said.

"I'm glad he said that he wanted everyone off there at all times. I called the office of the manager and they said that they were going to spread that topsoil tomorrow— if it didn't rain."

Theresa kept thinking. Mrs. Chinton looked and acted as she had every other day. When she picked up the pile of Sunday papers, Theresa glanced to see if she had been reading the apartment section.

She hadn't. Mrs. Chinton asked, "Is there anything in the paper you want to read?"

"I just remembered about a famous man. Dr. King. Can I find out more about him?"

Mrs. Chinton laughed. "I guess so. What would you want to find out? Maybe your brothers could give you the information you want."

Theresa told her about the Sunday meeting she had attended with Val. "The minister talked about making signs and marching and he said lots of other things. I was trying to remember." Theresa cleared the table. Her face was hidden behind the cabinet as she talked.

"Peaceful resistance, his movement is called," said Mrs. Chinton. "People sit down and let the world see what is happening. I've seen demonstrators doing that on television."

"Oh, yes," Theresa cried. "I remember now. Bye, Mother. Bye. I've got to go now." She knew exactly what she had to do.

She did not wait for the elevator. She ran down the seven flights of stairs in record time. Julie and Jonathan were arguing near the door of the back passageway.

"I've got it!" she called to them. "I know how to stop the fight."

Jonathan took one look at her and turned. "Don't!" he shouted and dashed down the passageway that led to the laundry rooms.

"Jonny's going to fight. None of the boys are going to school after lunch. They're going to get ammunition . . ."

"Let's go after Jonny," Theresa cried. "Come on, Julie. I know a way to stop the fight. Let's go . . ."

Fourteen

Julie dragged Theresa into a stairwell. They could talk there without being overheard. Theresa tugged on Julie's arm. Dena found them before the door could shut.

"Let's go. We haven't any time to lose," Theresa begged.

"Tell us first," Dena said

Theresa told them about sit-down strikes. "Dr. King was a great man and he said they work. He said you make big signs and everybody sees what is wrong. Then they fix it. We can write about Bert. Everyone will read the signs. Bert will be shamed forever."

"I've seen demonstrations on TV," Julie said. "Where will you sit down?"

"On the topsoil hill. Where they're going to fight. Only we won't fight. We'll sit down and hold signs like the grown-ups do on TV."

Dena whistled through her teeth. Julie hopped with excitement. "Will they do it? Oh, will everyone agree to sit down?"

"Let's try." Dena opened the stairwell door.

"It's our only chance. I called but Mr. Dyson and Miss Wilner were not in," Julie said. "I had to talk fast so Mother wouldn't hear me, but I think the secretary got the name right."

"Then, please let's go . . ."

Theresa had left her books in school, as had the other girls. They came out of the building the back way. No children were on this path. It led away from the school.

Dena fretted about being late for school. Theresa tripped over her own feet. She giggled nervously. "Imagine me not wanting to miss school!" She hurried after Dena.

Julie was first, ahead of Dena. She was making plans for the sit-down strike and almost in the same breath was talking about the operetta and Christmas vacation.

"Gee, Tweedy, if this works, maybe your mother will let you join the club. When Miss Wilner comes, we can get her to talk to your mother. Maybe we can invite Miss Wilner and Mr. Dyson to the operetta . . . and your friend from Harlem, the one that told you about Dr. King, and the rest of her family."

Dena pushed Julie ahead of her. "If you talked less,

you could walk faster. Hurry. We've got to get to the station parking lot fast."

The line-up buzzer sounded just as they reached the parking lot. They were southeast of the school and could hear the sudden quiet that followed the buzzer.

Julie stopped behind a car. "Too late," she said. "Look over there. There's a hundred of them."

Theresa gaped. Dozens of boys and girls were scampering around under the elevated railroad tracks. They were picking up stones and throwing them in bags and boxes. She heard the plunk of the stones as they fell. She could never talk to so many strangers. She had not counted on this crowd.

Dena prodded her. "Well, let's go."

"I can't . . ."

Dena stamped her foot. "You have to. We're late for school and we have to do something to make it worth while being late for. Come on."

Theresa began to sweat. Her eyes grew misty. Her legs buckled.

"Tweedy, listen to me," Dena scolded. "You can't freeze now. Remember that this may mean a new foster home. Remember that it means Julie never gets a chance to be on a real stage. Remember it means that we, all of us black kids, can't go where we want to in this neighborhood. Tweedy, are you listening?"

Theresa nodded. She touched Julie's face. It was wet. "Julie . . ." Theresa sucked a mouthful of air into her lungs. "Julie, are you crying?"

Julie nodded. Theresa ran her fingers over the warm tears. "I'll do it. For you."

"But I'm crying because I don't want you to go to another foster home. I want you to be happy like I am."

"Let's get moving," Dena begged.

Theresa threw her arms around Julie. Julie hugged her. "It's like being cousins," Julie cried. "We have Miss Wilner for our aunt and Mr. Dyson for our uncle, and maybe you can share Timmy and I can share your brothers when they come home . . ."

"Will you move?"

Theresa looked at Dena and wondered why she had ever thought Dena frog-faced. Dena stood tall. Her head was up, and her blunt nose and wide lips seemed carved out of ebony. She looked powerful—like a mighty statue.

Theresa flexed her legs. She thought of Miss Wilner's kitten. "I'm not scared. I'm not scared," she said to herself as she began to run through the parking lot to the clearing where the boys and girls were gathered.

"Jonny. Bob. Sharon. Hattie. We need you," Dena shouted.

"Jonny. Bob. Sharon. Hattie," Julie and Theresa echoed.

Julie fell on top of a rock-filled box. "Jonny," she yelled with increased strength.

Everyone gathered around Dena. Her voice filled the clearing. Jonny and Bob came forward together.

"Tweedy has a plan. She learned about it in Harlem. The most famous black man in the whole wide world used it. Someone told it to her. Come over here and listen."

Sharon made a face. "Do you know that Bert and his

gang are over near the church grounds getting ready to fight? We sent him a challenge."

"Good." Dena said. "That's what our plan is about."

Theresa was pushed into the middle of the group. A few kids yelled, "Fight first. Talk later."

Dena yelled them down and made Theresa talk louder. "You keep quiet," Dena told the boys. "For you this is only a fight about pride. You have to pay Bert back for Kenneth. Well listen to me, bozos, for Tweedy this is a fight for more than pride. It's a fight for her home. Get it—H-O-M-E."

Julie held her hands. Dena was at her shoulder. Jonathan was in front of her looking down at her.

Theresa found words to tell her story and her plan. At first no one said anything. Then a boy said the idea was "corny." Another boy said he had heard about Dr. King on TV. He did not think much of sitting down as a way of fighting. He wanted to fight standing up as some of the other big Negro leaders did.

Hattie wondered how they would make signs. Sharon began by laughing at Hattie and ended up by saying, "You know, it's just crazy enough to work. Bert is expecting a fight. He'll come with his rocks. He's always saying that we lie about him . . ."

Bob jumped high in the air. "He'll get caught in his lie. We'll have the signs and he'll have the ammunition."

Theresa could not talk any more. Julie was laughing and crying at the same time. She had squeezed Theresa's hand so hard that Theresa's fingers were numb.

Hattie patted her hair down before she asked, "So where are we going to get the signs?"

For an instant everyone stood open-mouthed and silent. Then Julie cried out, "From Mrs. Jennet. Let's tell her. Let's tell all the teachers and the principal. Let's tell them so that they can catch Bert and his gang with their ammunition in their hands."

Telling the teachers wasn't popular, but since no one had a better plan it was agreed that Julie and Theresa and Dena be delegated to talk to Mrs. Jennet. The other children in the other classes would wait to see what the girls came back with.

"We can always fight Bert some other day if he doesn't quit bugging us," Bob said to Jonathan. "This trick on him will pay him back for all the dirty ones he played on us."

Julie was at the school door when she heard Bob's remark. Her face reddened. "Gee, it's a dirty trick to play. Maybe we ought not to—I don't like being dirty . . ."

Dena poked her. "Too late. It's trick or fight. An early Halloween."

Dena went into the classroom first. All heads turned toward her. Paul almost jumped out of his seat when he saw her.

Theresa and Julie peeped in through the door. Bert and his friends weren't in class. Dena and Mrs. Jennet talked fast. Mrs. Jennet wet her lips time and time again. She came to the door with Dena.

"You girls come in. I'm sending Dena down to the principal. But I can't promise that he won't send for your mothers."

"Then we're going out of here right now," Julie said.

"I thought you'd be with us. Do you want Tweedy to lose her home, just when we found each other?"

Mrs. Jennet wrung her hands. She bit on her lips. "It's breaking a school law. I cannot let this go on . . ."

"Would you rather see a fight?"

Mrs. Jennet dropped her eyes before Dena dropped hers.

Mrs. Jennet began to smile. "Dena, someday you'll be a lawyer like your father. You argue a good case even now."

Julie ran down to let in the other girls and boys. Mrs. Jennet sent Paul to each of the children's teachers with a note. When he came back, Mrs. Jennet told the class everything that Dena had told her.

"We have asked the teachers to excuse all the children involved. Now I will allow all who wish to make signs and prepare a program of peaceful demonstration to stay in this room."

The class and the visitors from other rooms began to work fast and quietly. Magic Markers were brought out. Construction paper was lined and cut. Someone found a picture of Dr. King in an old magazine. He cut it out and pasted it on a sign.

Many of the boys and girls wanted to join the sit-down strike. Mrs. Jennet said they had to go home and talk to their mothers first.

"This is not as easy as it sounds," she said to Jonathan and Bob. "If you're right—and Bert's absence indicates that you may be right—then Bert's friends will be coming with rocks and sticks. What's to prevent him from throwing them?"

Julie stood up. "That's what he'll do. He's a coward and a rat. If he doesn't throw any, then we've got him pegged wrong."

Bob snickered. "He'll throw them all right. If he sees only us, he'll throw for sure."

Julie stopped printing her sign. "Mrs. Jennet, let's see if he does. Promise not to tell the principal or do anything until three-thirty. Promise?"

Mrs. Jennet did not like to make that promise. But at last she did. "I can't believe that such a sweet-looking boy could be so vicious," she said as the class lined up the signs for inspection.

"Freedom for All."

"This Land is My Land."

"We'll sit here all we like."

"No one can get away with breaking bones."

"Be on our side—be democratic."

Theresa's experience in hat trimming was coming in handy. She put a streamer here, a button there.

In the back of the room, Jonathan was leading a group in some singing. He planned to sing "America" and several other patriotic songs. He hoped lots of people would hear the singing and come out to see the signs.

"We want a great big crowd," he said.

Julie giggled. "I made a sign advertising our club and our operetta. Tweedy, it's going to be great."

Mrs. Jennet was more nervous than anyone else. She went to talk to the other teachers before the bell rang. "Jonathan," she said as he got in line, "I wish you all luck. I'm afraid I've been rather unfair. It was hard

to believe that Bert, with his honest blue eyes, could be lying."

The bell rang and the class and the visitors got in line. Mrs. Jennet looked heavenward. "I pray I haven't done wrong. Bless you," she whispered.

Theresa and the girls left their books in school. They took only their signs and moved toward the outside door. Theresa felt Mrs. Jennet touch her. "No one in their right mind would let anything take you away from them. Don't worry, child. Your foster parents will never let you go . . . even if they move . . . I feel it in my heart."

As they reached the yard, Jonathan stuck his hand out. "Shake, Mrs. Jennet, for luck."

Theresa wanted to cry. Everyone was so kind. Everyone was looking to her for ideas . . . praising her . . . *If only her foster mother would change her mind about people. If only her foster mother could see Paul, Jennie, Julie, and some of the other white kids working for the strike.*

"Dad isn't afraid of white people being rude," Theresa said to Julie as if she were Mrs. Chinton, who was at home preparing dinner. "Why won't you try—just try for his sake and for mine?"

She felt a tiny pinch. "Wake up, Tweedy. Stop dreaming. We're on our way. We're ready."

"I'm ready, too," Theresa said and took her sign under her arm. It read, "We need each other."

Fifteen

We need each other, Theresa kept saying to herself as she walked silently out of the school yard with the other silent children.

"Give us fifteen minutes, Mrs. Jennet, before you tell the principal," Dena whispered.

Nothing about the next fifteen minutes was ordinary. Children going home were either unnaturally quiet or exceptionally shrill. Some ran, heads down and eyes darting from side to side. Others dawdled near the school gate, far enough from the topsoil hill to be safe, yet close enough to see.

Theresa found that breathing was extra hard.

No one said "trouble," but everyone felt it coming. Theresa pressed her sign against her body to stop herself from shaking.

Some boys from behind parked cars began a chant:

Blacks go back to Africa,
We don't need you here.

The short walk to the topsoil hill seemed miles long. Theresa kept in the center of the group, between Sharon and Dena. She wondered if the girls could hear how loudly her heart was beating.

It was not until she was sitting up on top of the hill where Dena had put her that Theresa saw how many children were participating in the sit-down strike. Thirty, or more. Mostly Negro boys and girls.

There was a brisk wind blowing and Theresa was glad to be surrounded by children. They had brought newspapers with them from the classroom and were now sitting on them. The girls were up high and the boys closer to the ground.

"Just in case . . . " Bob said ominously.

"Please . . . you promised not to fight," Theresa moaned.

"Who said he's going to fight?" Sharon asked.

"All I'm going to do is protect myself and you girls," Bob replied as he settled his sign against his knees.

"I wish some grown-ups would come around," Hattie whispered. "I don't like the way it's gotten so quiet."

It was then that Theresa realized that the voices from behind the parked cars had stopped. It was then that she realized how alone and defenseless they were. Even the wind seemed to be blowing harder.

From the far end of the parking lot, she heard a shrill insistent whistle. "Signs up, everyone. They're coming," Jonathan cried.

Running toward her, Theresa saw dozens of boys, swinging sticks and ropes around their heads. They advanced shouting filthy names and threats.

A wave of dizziness came over her. *Why did I think this strike would make Mother like white people? What if she comes and sees us all getting killed? What will happen now?* she thought as she gripped her sign more firmly.

Closer and closer the voices came whooping and shouting. Suddenly one clear note rang over the hill. It was Jonathan singing. "Deep in my heart . . . I do believe . . ."

Dena's contralto took up the tune. Soon, one by one, every voice was joined in song. As Theresa sang, she took Sharon's hand and Hattie's hand. She held them knowing that they were holding other hands.

Pebbles and bits of garbage flew past her. Theresa did not move. She heard an "ouch." Someone had been hit. She was glad that Julie was not on the hill—glad that Julie had been picked to tell the mothers where they were.

Please, dear God, she prayed. *Let them hit only me. Please don't let anyone else get hurt.*

She stood up. All alone she stood up on the hill inviting the Dukes to aim for her. They were coming from behind the trees, the shopping center, the parked cars.

The Dukes were coming closer, but the singing did not falter. The song rang out clearly through the parking lot and over the paths and the whole area.

Theresa saw people coming from the buildings. Many people. "Down, Theresa, sit down," a voice screamed at her.

Automatically, Theresa plopped down in her place. Sharon pulled her to one side and held her there. "Want them to aim at you?" Sharon asked. "What did you stand up for?"

"Come down from there, Theresa."

Theresa wiped the mist from her eyes. "Mother," she shrieked, "go away, you'll get hurt."

Other names were being called. Mothers were swarming toward the topsoil hill chasing the white boys. Mrs. Chinton was pressing through the crowd.

A white woman stopped her. "Wait. Don't panic. We don't want anyone hurt."

Theresa saw Julie slithering between the people who were trying to get to the hill and the strikers without getting hit with the rotten vegetables.

"Tweedy!" Julie yelled. "Tweedy, I'm back with a million people."

To Theresa it looked like a million people. She gasped. The singing stopped. Mrs. Shinerman was holding all the grown-ups back as she had held back Mrs. Chinton.

"You cowards," she was shouting at the white boys. "Stop throwing that stuff. Stop, before I call the police. Beat it, hear me!"

The attackers snickered, but halted.

Mrs. Shinerman was forming a ring around the hill. "If you don't go away fast, we'll block you off and you'll stay here till the cops come!"

"Come, folks," Mrs. Shinerman was calling at the top of her lungs. "Come help us protect our children."

From far off a siren sounded. Just then Mrs. Jennet came running from the school yard with the principal. "Get those boys," she said to the people on the paths.

Like rabbits, the attackers bounded away from the hill and made for the paths leading from the school.

"Look at them go!"

"We won!"

"We won!"

"Good riddance."

"It worked, Tweedy. It worked." Julie jumped up. She hugged Sharon and Hattie and Theresa. "The strike is over," she sang. "It's over."

Mrs. Jennet came up on the hill. "Ladies and gentlemen," she said through the loudspeaker she was carrying. "We have given the police the names of the boys concerned in this fight. But I think you ought to know the story of this sit-down strike."

With the principal's help, Mrs. Jennet had a few of the children talk through the loudspeaker. Jonathan told about Bert's threats and the challenge to fight.

Julie told about Theresa's part in the strike. Theresa grew so hot while Julie talked that she had to unbutton her coat.

When the story had been told, Mrs. Shinerman stood near Mrs. Jennet. "This topsoil hill will be removed tomorrow, but the fighting will not stop with that, unless all of us here do something to bring peace."

The grown-ups were standing huddled together against the cold. Theresa saw more white faces than brown or black ones. Where had they all come from? On the hill were many children who lived outside the cooperative. Most of the people listening to Mrs. Shinerman probably had no children in the strike. Yet they were listening and nodding while Mrs. Shinerman talked about the civic club and the junior club.

Julie forgot to cover her mouth while she smiled and smiled. Theresa had to smile with her. Bob was folding up his sign and congratulating Dena.

Why did I ever think Dena had a frog-face? Theresa wondered again. *She's almost pretty when she laughs.*

The principal organized parents to escort the strikers home. "I don't trust those boys not to re-form their attack when they feel it's safe," he said.

The good-bys were loud and joyous. The principal promised that Bert's parents would be visited by a committee of parents and that he would be with them. Each boy who had participated in the attack on the topsoil hill would be identified and punished.

"Sit-down strikes are fun!" Hattie said before Sharon could stop her.

Bob snorted. "Not from where I sat. I got most of the garbage."

Off they went joking. Theresa heard their voices long after they had disappeared from view. She kept close to Julie and Dena. Mrs. Chinton was right in the center of a group of white people who were asking questions about the clubs and the operetta.

Theresa saw Mrs. Chinton trying to get out of the crowd without pushing anyone. Her foster mother seemed eager to escape, yet unable to force her way out.

The white people around her seemed unaware of her discomfort.

Theresa wiggled her way into the circle around Mrs. Shinerman. "Come on, Mother," she whispered. "Follow me. I'll clear the way."

Just as she had Mrs. Chinton faced in the right direction, two things happened. Mrs. Shinerman grabbed for Mrs. Chinton's arm, and Mr. Chinton began calling, "Marjorie. Theresa. Where are you?"

In a few seconds Mrs. Shinerman had the crowd quiet. "For information, call these numbers," she said and she handed Julie a list of telephone numbers that people might copy.

"Please don't run away, Mrs. Chinton," Mrs. Shinerman begged. "Let us walk back together."

"Marge!"

"I'm here with Mrs. Shinerman," Mrs. Chinton called.

"Here, Dad," Theresa called. "Here, near the topsoil hill. We're here. Mother's waiting for Mrs. Shinerman."

"Thank God, you're safe." Mr. Chinton hugged Theresa. He took Mrs. Chinton's arm and held it. "I heard the commotion and ran home. I never thought to find you two out *here*."

"Nor did I . . ." a booming voice said.

Everyone turned to look at the stout woman puffing into the parking lot.

"Miss Wilner."

Julie and Theresa ran together.

"Miss Wilner," called Julie, "we had a sit-down strike and we won, and now Mrs. Chinton is going to be friends with some white people and . . ."

"I'm not so sure," Theresa said to Miss Wilner as the social worker cried, "Julie, slow down and tell me the whole story."

"Tell it to all of us, girls," Mrs. Shinerman said. The crowd had gone. Only Jonathan, Dena, and the two girls were left with the Chintons and Mrs. Shinerman.

"Come up in my house. I left Timmy in Mrs. Thompson's house," Mrs. Shinerman said apologetically. "When Julie came home to tell us, Jonny's mother and I thought it better for me to go . . . because I'm white and Bert might respond better to me . . ."

Shyly, Mrs. Chinton walked between Mr. Chinton and Mrs. Shinerman. Theresa could not take her eyes off her foster mother. In spite of all the compliments she had received, she did not know what her foster mother was going to do.

"Don't be glum." Julie fixed a smile on Theresa's face with her fingers. "Miss Wilner, tell Tweedy not to be such a worrier."

"I'm afraid telling doesn't help," the social worker answered. "Look at me, I'm forever worrying."

Since Miss Wilner refused to hear one word of the story until everyone was listening, Julie wanted to know how she had happened to come today.

"I called about one o'clock and asked your mothers if they were going to be home," the social worker explained. "Only when I got to your homes, no one was there to greet me. Luckily, Mrs. Thompson heard me ring the bell and she told me where you all were."

"I think you'll be taking me with you," Theresa said softly.

"Really?" Miss Wilner raised her brows. "I thought you might like it here. And now that I see you and Julie have met, I'm sorry to hear you want to go."

"She doesn't WANT to go!" Julie exclaimed. "And I'm sure she won't have to . . . because . . ."

Miss Wilner did not hear the end of the story. Dena wanted to say good-by, and Mrs. Chinton insisted that she had to go to her own house to begin dinner.

Then Mr. Chinton invited Mrs. Shinerman, Jonathan, and Julie up to their apartment.

"I'll pick up Timmy and come up in a few minutes," Mrs. Shinerman said, her eyes on Mrs. Chinton. "That is, if you're sure I won't be in the way."

Theresa held her breath. Mrs. Chinton seemed to be having trouble swallowing. When it seemed that she would never talk again, she suddenly cleared her throat and said to her husband, "Mrs. Shinerman took a big risk out there . . . She made all those people come around and protect our children from those hoodlums . . . I don't know what might have happened if she had not been there to organize a defense . . ."

Theresa thought she would burst with pride. Mrs. Shinerman was blushing. She was saying, "It was really the least I could do . . . Really anybody would . . ."

"Will someone please hurry and tell me the story," Miss Wilner cried. "I'm dying of curiosity and I hate to wait for anything."

In the elevator Theresa clung to Mrs. Chinton's arm. In the apartment she set a pot of coffee on to boil. Then she quickly showed Miss Wilner her new blouse and her two ivy plants.

"This healthy one is my mother's," she said. "It has a new sprout and has grown an inch and a half."

"I guess good soil and good care makes a tremendous difference in plants," Miss Wilner said thoughtfully. She listened to Theresa's ideas for the other science projects in her class.

"Have you written to the Gardiners yet?" she asked. "One of the reasons I was anxious to see you was because Val Gardiner called Mr. Dyson to ask how you were."

Stumblingly, Theresa found words to tell why she had not written. "I wanted to be sure I was staying . . . I had to be sure . . ."

"Perhaps you can invite them to visit you during Christmas vacation?"

"That would be nice," Theresa answered. "Val wants to meet my family. The boys . . . my brothers write me letters. I think they will like Val and the Gardiners."

The door bell rang. "Open the door, Theresa," Mrs. Chinton called.

Jonathan and his mother and baby brother came in, followed by Mrs. Shinerman, Julie, and Timmy. Quite a party listened to the story.

The grown-ups had coffee and the children drank milk. Miss Wilner shook her head admiringly. "My, you certainly kept your promise to me. If I had kept mine as well, I'd be the merest shadow of myself by this time."

Theresa sprang to Miss Wilner's defense. "I had a lot of help. Julie and Jonny did as much for the strike as I did. If Julie hadn't brought the grown-ups, we might have been licked."

"But we won, and I think we're going to have lots of

new club members, and the operetta will be a great, big, wonderful success," Julie sang out.

"Can Tweedy join?" Jonathan asked.

"Please," Mrs. Shinerman said. "And we truly wish you would help us as much as you can. We have to stay together. The *Bert's* of this world will never change."

Mr. Chinton smiled at Theresa. In a voice only she could hear he whispered, "I guess Mother's been transplanted today. It will take a while for roots to grow . . ."

Theresa took her foster father's hand. She still got a peculiar feeling in her chest when she looked around this room. Would she ever feel she belonged entirely?

Silently she motioned to Julie. They went into her room and stood near her pot of ivy. "I bought this for my mother before she died," she said. "It seems to like living here."

Julie pressed her hands around Theresa's. They exchanged no words but together they returned to the living room. It was time to go home.

Miss Wilner would be back to see the play. "I'll try to lose at least five pounds by then," she said with determination.

"No matter how you look, we'll be glad to see you," Mr. Chinton said. "You and Mr. Dyson have done a lot for all of us."

"And Dr. Martin Luther King, too," Theresa added.

The smile on Mrs. Chinton's face grew deeper and brighter. Theresa shut the door after her friends and went into the kitchen humming. She was already making up the letter she would write to the Gardiners. She knew exactly what to say.

ABOUT THE AUTHOR

Betty Baum, a teacher trained in the All-Day Neighborhood School Program in New York City, is a graduate of Hunter College. In her first book, PATRICIA CROSSES TOWN, *a young Negro girl is bussed to an integrated school and learns, slowly and sometimes painfully, that people are very much alike, regardless of the color of their skin.* A NEW HOME FOR THERESA *is her second book for Knopf. Mrs. Baum, a mother and a grandmother, lives in Jamaica, Long Island.*

Text set in Linotype Baskerville
Composed and bound by The Book Press, Inc., Brattleboro, Vermont
Printed by Halliday Lithograph Corp., West Hanover, Massachusetts
Typography by Atha Tehon